Music Express

Foundation stage FS

LEARNING INTENTIONS, ACTIVITIES, SONGS, STORIES, PICTURES, RECORDINGS, VIDEOCLIPS

Series devised by **Maureen Hanke**

Compiled by **Sue Nicholls** and **Patricia Scott** with **Sally Hickman**

Illustrated by **Alison Dexter**   Edited by **Sheena Roberts**

Audio CDs produced by **Stephen Chadwick**

Videoclips produced by **Alan Long**

A & C Black • London

Contents

First published 2003
A&C Black Publishers Ltd
37 Soho Square, London W1D 3QZ
© 2003 A&C Black Publishers Ltd

Teaching text © 2003 Sue Nicholls and Patricia Scott
  with Sally Hickman
Book compilation © 2003 A&C Black Publishers Ltd
CD/Videoclips compilation © 2003 A&C Black Publishers Ltd
Edited by Sheena Roberts
Designed by Jocelyn Lucas
Cover illustration © 2002 Alex Ayliffe
Inside illustrations © 2003 Alison Dexter
Audio CD sound engineering by Stephen Chadwick
Videoclips filmed and edited by Alan Long Services
Videoclip script written and presented by Sally Hickman
Music setting by Jeanne Fisher
CD-ROM post production by Ian Shepherd
  at Sound Recording Technology

Printed in Great Britain by Caligraving Ltd, Thetford, Norfolk

A&C Black uses paper produced with elemental chlorine-free
pulp, harvested from managed sustainable forests.

A CIP catalogue record for this book is available from the
British Library.

Introduction

About Music Express

The *Music Express* series provides activities that are imaginative, inspiring and fun. The series has been written especially for classroom teachers and early years practitioners. It is:

- user-friendly;
- well planned;
- fully resourced, and
- no music reading is required.

Using Music Express FS

National Curriculum

Music Express FS has been written to support the QCA Curriculum Guidance for the Foundation Stage in England. The guidance is divided into six areas of learning, which are common to the Foundation Stages in Scotland, Northern Ireland and Wales. The *Music Express FS* activities are intended to be delivered to support holistic learning and to provide learning opportunities in more than one area.

The units

The activities are divided into units, corresponding to the six focused areas of learning given in the Guidance:

- Personal, social and emotional development;
- Communication, language and literacy;
- Mathematical development;
- Knowledge and understanding of the world;
- Physical development;
- Creative development.

Within each unit the activities are arranged in six further sections, each containing four developmental stages, which link with the Guidance.

QCA's Curriculum Guidance shows practitioners how most children will develop through Stepping Stones towards Early Learning Goals at the end of Foundation Stage. In the Guidance, the Stepping Stones are coloured yellow, blue and green. The initial yellow Stepping Stone will show practitioners what a child's learning will look like as it enters the Foundation Stage, and how it might progress through the blue and green Stepping Stones before reaching the grey Early Learning Goal.

Each unit also has a musical focus, featuring one of the elements of music:

- Beat and tempo;
- High and low;
- Structure;
- Texture;
- Loud and quiet;
- Timbre.

The musical focus offers a bridge between Foundation Stage and the KS1 Music Curriculum.

Some sections use one activity as a starting point from which to progress through all the developmental stages (yellow – grey). Others have more than one, offering the enrichment and broadening of the children's learning through a wider variety of material.

The Foundation Stage –

- supports a shared language and mutual valuing of everyone working with children;

- refers to all those working with children as practitioners and the place in which they work as the setting;

- is a child-centred, active and holistic curriculum in which teaching and learning is delivered through play;

- is based on the theories of child development and is a progressive curriculum;

- acknowledges that the children's parents are their first and most enduring educators and should be valued and encouraged to be involved in their children's learning and development;

- caters for the individual needs of the child, building on what the child already knows and can do, and extending their learning and interests;

- should provide a balance of indoor and outdoor experiences for the children, wherever possible allowing children's learning to take place outside;

- requires the children to be observed, their learning evaluated and this information used in the planning of their next steps.

By observing and recording children's learning during their participation in the activities in this book, practitioners will be supported in making judgements about the individual child's development when completing the Foundation Stage Profile.

The Foundation Stage Profile is a statutory assessment which takes place at the end of the

Foundation Stage. The Profile is intended to show what the child can do in all the six areas of learning. The learning is measured by practitioners using on-going records and observations collected through the child's time in the Foundation Stage. This picture of the whole child will be shared with the parents, who will also have helped by sharing information about their child. The Profile is then used as a basis on which to plan the child's next steps as they move into Key Stage 1.

In *Music Express FS* any reference made to children by gender should be taken to mean all children. Likewise reference made to parents means parents, carers or the person with legal responsibility for the child or children.

Music in the Foundation Stage

The activities may take place at any time during the session, and may involve individuals, pairs, small or large groups.

It is intended that the units and activities are approached through a dip-in two-year rolling programme.

It is not intended that each unit should be taught over a half term, nor in the order in which they appear. Instead activities might be chosen in response to child-initiated learning. For instance a child or group of children might be exploring snow and ice, in which case the practitioner may turn to the activities on *Winter* in *Growth and change*. Within that set of activities, the practitioner chooses the level (yellow – grey) appropriate to the children's stage of development, whether general or musical.

Alternatively, a practitioner may identify from an activity that they can plan for a new stage of development for some or all of the children.

Essentially, the activities are intended to form an integral part of a child-centred, active, holistic curriculum and are best-suited to a dip-in approach.

Content

The CD-ROM

– unit overviews

The CD-ROM provides overviews of each unit, which may be printed out for easy access. These break down into more detail the learning which is taking place.

Whilst it is not necessary when teaching the activities to have the overviews alongside, they contain useful information for generalist practitioners, including:

- Foundation Stage learning intentions;

- musical learning and activity content;
- a glossary of musical terms;

– picture gallery

Colour illustrations for most units are included and may be printed out to use as extra stimulus for an activity. Two of these colour illustrations are interactive and are intended to be used by the children themselves. Other resources in the gallery include mask templates or other visuals to print out onto card.

– story texts

There are several stories in the book, which are recorded in full on the CDs and are available as text on the CD-ROM.

– melody lines

While all the songs are provided on, and may be learned from the CD, music readers will find all the melody lines available in staff notation on the CD-ROM.

– videoclips

See section below.

The book

This provides step-by-step instructions for delivering each activity.

Preparation time should include reading all the levels for the section you wish to use. You will find:

- a resource list, including visuals, instruments and soundmakers you may need;
- a set of icons which indicate what you need to have available.

Key to icons

 CD-ROM picture gallery icon: you will need access to a computer to view or print a picture.

 CD icon: there are two CDs. The track numbering begins from one again in the section *Working world*.

 Videoclip icon: you will need access to a computer to view videoclips. p clips are for the practitioner to view, as the instrument demonstrations; c clips are for the children.

 Outdoor or large space icon: - these indicate when an activity is particularly suited to a large space inside or out of doors.

 Story icon: you will need access to a computer in order to view or print a story text on the CD-ROM.

Tune starting notes

The first few notes of every melody are given next to its appearance in the book as a quick reminder of how each song begins, and as a guide to the pitch which will be comfortable for the children to sing.

Other resources

Instruments and everyday sound sources

You will need to have available a range of percussion instruments and environmental soundmakers.

Specific activities recommend the instruments you will need, but you should use the instruments that you have available.

For a setting, aim to have at least the following:

Tuned percussion

1 alto xylophone

a selection of beaters

A range of untuned percussion, eg

tambours and hand drums

wood blocks and claves

maracas and cabasas

jingle bells and tambourines

guiros

rainmakers and chocolos

Help for practitioners

Tips, extensions and background information

These are provided throughout and are next to the activity or activities to which they refer.

Teaching songs

We hope that you will lead the singing with your own voice, but in all instances we have allowed for the use of the CD.

If you feel confident, teach yourself a song using the CD and then teach it to the children.

Children of this age range benefit from whole song teaching, rather than breaking a song into small sections. Sing the song complete with accompanying actions, encouraging the children to join in with you as it becomes familiar. This may mean that some children will join in with actions only at first, while others will sing individual words or phrases. At this age it is natural that movement and song go together. As their confidence grows, so will their ability to perform the entire song with all the actions.

Videoclips

Clips p1–p23

These practitioners' videoclips demonstrate one complete section of activities from each unit in progress from yellow through to grey.

The videoclips show children in real learning situations, sometimes demonstrating the same level of development, sometimes showing that responses may be differentiated, eg yellow and grey responses may be seen to be happening within the same activity.

These have been filmed in normal learning situations, and give a true representation of what you might expect to meet in using the material.

The videoclips provide the practitioner with an overview of how these activities work in different settings with children of different ages and at individual stages of development. The delivery and organisation have been interpreted from the book by the individual practitioners and show different styles of teaching and learning.

The commentary which accompanies the videoclips provides information on the musical learning and levels the children are working at.

Clips c1–c5

These are for the children to view. They offer an initial stimulus to some of the activities.

Instrument clips

The instrument videoclips show some common, untuned percussion in use as a quick reference for practitioners, who may feel less confident about handling and playing these instruments.

Further learning

A&C Black website

Music Express FS provides all the resources you will need for two years of music making. We hope, however, that you will use other songs and activities in subsequent years.

The website www.acblack.com/musicexpress lists the *Music Express FS* activities that were drawn from or inspired by other A&C Black books, and links to other books that will supplement the activities in *Music Express FS.*

Acknowledgements

The authors and publishers are grateful to the following copyright holders for their permission to include their copyright works in *Music Express Foundation Stage*:

Chinese New Year reproduced by permission of Mrs Low Siew Poh, licensed on her behalf by: Educational Publications Bureau Pte Ltd 3545C Blk 162 Bukit Merah Central Singapore.
The clock goes tick tock, © 1991 Mavis de Mierre.
Hello, Mr Sun, © 1997 Niki Davies.
Ghoom–parani gaan, © Monju Majid.
I hear the band, © Sue Nicholls.
The Iron Man (extract) by Ted Hughes from Faber Children's Classics. Used by permission of Faber & Faber, 3 Queen Square, London WC1N 3AU.
Jack-in-the-box (from *Singing Sherlock*), © Sue Nicholls.
Say hello by Maggie Anwell, Tony Coult, John Rust and Charlie Stafford; *Make a face* by George Dewey and *How do you do?* by ED Berman, all from *Game-Songs with Prof Dogg's Troupe*, created by ED Berman, published by A&C Black Publishers Limited. Used by permission.
Rainbow dreams (also known as *First light*), © Pamela Marre.
The snow is dancing (from *Children's Corner Suite* by Claude Debussy), courtesy of Deutsche Gramaphon. Licensed by kind permission from the Film & TV Licensing Division, part of the Universal Music Group.

The following copyright material has been created for *Music Express Foundation Stage*:

Ananse, Puss and Ratta retold by Jan Blake. *Dumplings* (story) by Jan Blake, created for *Music Express Foundation Stage*, © 2003.
A dragon moves like this, Brer Ananse Spider, Cake for tea, Dragon swoops, I've got a tambour, Litter bag, Litter muncher, Paper poem, Play it change it, Shake, tappety, scrape, What can you hear? When we're on the farm, What can you hear when you wake up yawning? What can you play? – all by Patricia Scott, created for *Music Express Foundation Stage*, © 2003.
Caterpillar caterpillar, Fish swim - birds fly, Friends in the middle, The Jack factory, Jumping high, The king's birthday music, Music market, My turn your turn, Our tap drips, Popcorn, Prowl and growl, Sound parade, Sky-high toe-low, Storm, Who has the pebble? – all by Sue Nicholls, created for *Music Express Foundation Stage*, © 2003.
Dragon swoops (music) by Helen East and Rick Wilson, created for *Music Express Foundation Stage*, © 2003.
Four fat dumplings by Sue Nicholls and Jan Blake, created for *Music Express Foundation Stage*, © 2003.
Foxy comes to town and *The little toymaker* by Kaye Umansky, created for *Music Express Foundation Stage*, © 2003.
The Jack factory (music), *Bear's waking up dance, Stormy sky dance, Ghost dance, Rainbow dreams* (music) by Stephen Chadwick, created for *Music Express Foundation Stage*, © 2003.
The magic dove by Helen East, created for *Music Express Foundation Stage*, © 2003.

The following copyright material has been published previously in A&C Black publications:

Dee-di-diddle-o by Veronica Clark from *High low dolly pepper*, published by A&C Black Publishers Limited, © 1991.

Don't drop litter, I have sounds one and two, I'm walking like a robot, There's a tiny caterpillar on a leaf from *Bobby Shaftoe clap your hands* by Sue Nicholls, published by A&C Black Publishers Limited, © 1992.
Hairy Scary Castle from *Three Singing Pigs*, published by A&C Black Publishers Limited, © 1994.
My machine from *Bingo lingo* by Helen MacGregor, published by A&C Black Publishers Limited, © 1999.
Please, Mr Noah from *Three Tapping Teddies* by Kaye Umansky, published by A&C Black Publishers Limited, © 2000.
Stamp and clap, Supermarket song, Five wonky bicycles from *Tom Thumb's Musical Maths* by Helen MacGregor, published by A&C Black Publishers Limited, © 1997.
What can you see? by Sue Nicholls from *Songbirds: Me*, published by A&C Black Publishers Limited, © 1997.

Videoclips

All practitioners' videoclips (p1–p23) and instrument videoclips, and the children's videoclips of *Jack-in-the-box* and *Rainbow* were filmed and edited by Alan Long Services (tel: 01775 712260, email: alanlongservices@freenetname.co.uk) © 2003 A&C Black.
Chinese dragon, courtesy of BSkyB Ltd.
Marching band, © Alan Long Services.
Winter scene, © A&C Black.

Audio CD performances

Kevin Graal (voice)
Debbie Sanders (voice)
Jan Blake (voice - *Ananse, Puss and Ratta, Dumplings, Four fat dumplings, Brer Ananse Spider, Little Miss Muffet*)
Helen East (voice - *The magic dove*)
Monju Majid (voice - *Baak bakum paira, Ghoom-parani gaan*)
Steve Grocott (guitar, mandolin, banjo, harmonica)
Rick Wilson (percussion)
Stephen Chadwick (keyboards, synth)

Thanks also to performers of tracks used in previous A&C Black recordings - Sandra Kerr and Ben Parry (*Kye kye kule*), Helen Chadwick and Chris Larner (*Dee-di-diddle-o*)

Thanks

The authors and publishers extend thanks to all those who took part in the creation of *Music Express Foundation Stage*.

Particular thanks are due to the staff and children of the settings in which the videoclips were filmed: Featherstone Nursery (Muriel Halpin, Cathy Khurana and Mary Pearson); Christ Church CE Foundation Unit (Teresia Moriani, Melanie Davies and Mrs Basu); Ryhall Nursery and CE Primary School (Julie Beecham, Amanda Donelan, Linda Swann, Joyce Bull, Sandra Whittle, Jan Williams and Sue Steele).

Thanks also to: Maureen Hanke, Helen MacGregor, Carla Moss, Tania Demidova, Michelle Simpson, Marie Penny, Kate Davies, Jane Sebba, Jenny Fisher, Brian and Alice Nicholls, Keith and Thomas Scott, David, John and Amie-Rose Hickman.

Special people

Musical focus: Beat and tempo **Area of learning:** Personal, social and emotional development

YELLOW

VIDEOCLIPS
Reference clips of these YELLOW, BLUE, GREEN and GREY activities are included on the CD-ROM.

TUNE
D   E   G
Say   hel - lo

EXTENSION
Some children will be able to respond with 'hello' to their own names when the song is adapted like this:

Hello Jade
  Jade: Hello
Hello Rakesh
  Rakesh: Hello
Hello Alan
  Alan: Hello
Hello Abiola
  Abiola: Hello

Say hello

- Greet the children and their families as they come in by saying 'hello' and encouraging a 'hello' in response.

- Listen to *Say hello* (*track 1*), inviting the children to wave 'hello' with the responses:

Leader:	*Children:*
Say hello,	Hello,
Say hello,	Hello,
Say hello,	Hello,
Say hello,	Hello.

- Listen again and tap the beat on shoulders, on knees, or on the floor:

Say   hel - lo   Hel - lo ...

- Sing *Say hello* with or without the CD, encouraging the children to respond by waving and singing 'hello'.

BLUE

TUNE
A F♯ A D
How do you do?

TIP
The music on the CD is extended with instrumental repeats of the song to give extra time in which to shake hands.

Model the exchange of greetings with one of the children, inviting them to shake your hand to a steady beat while saying or singing 'How do you do?'

How do you do?

- Play *How do you do?* (*track 2*). Standing in a circle, the children join hands and swing them up and down as they listen, joining in with the echoed response when they are ready:

Leader:	*Children:*
How do you do?	How do you do?
I'm very pleased	I'm very pleased
to meet you.	to meet you.
How do you do?	How do you do?

- Turn to face a partner in the circle and repeat the activity, this time shaking hands to the steady beat of the song as you sing it or play the CD.

- Perform the song with or without the CD in a large space. During the song the children walk freely in several directions, stopping to greet each other by shaking hands and saying or singing, 'How do you do'. Ask the children if they have said 'How do you do' to a new friend.

Hello

GREEN

EXTENSION
The children may work in pairs, one child leading. The leader performs a sequence of greeting actions copied by his or her partner. Perform them with or without the song. Take turns to be leader.

How do you do signs

- Sing *How do you do* (track 2) with or without the CD, encouraging the children to respond with the echoed lines and by shaking hands with each other.

- Show the children other greeting actions, eg

    – fist with raised thumb, drawn across body from one side to the other (*hearing-impaired*);

    – palms together and head bowed (*India*);

    – kiss on alternate cheeks (*France*);

    – slap raised open palm against another's (*USA*).

- Choose a greeting action to perform as you sing the song:

Leader: How do you do?   *Children:* How do you do?

- To welcome parents into school at home time, the children might perform a sequence of different greeting actions during the song, following you or a child as leader.

GREY

RESOURCES
Ask parents to contribute to a display of pictures, clothing, foods and artifacts from different countries and cultures.

TUNE
A F♯ A D
We say bonjour

TIP
Ask parents' help to translate the whole song into other languages. (An Urdu and a Bengali version are given on videoclip P4.)

How else do you do?

- Sing *How do you do?* (track 2). Share and sing with the children greetings in various languages, eg

French:
We say bonjour,
We're very pleased
   to meet you,
We say bonjour,

We say bonjour,
We're very pleased
   to meet you,
We say bonjour.

Arabic/Urdu: We say asalaam a leikum...

Swahili: We say jambo...

Bengali: We say kamon acho...

Chinese: We say ni hao...

- Make a grand performance of the song at a special time such as Christmas, Eid, harvest, Baisakhi, or a world sporting event. Children welcome the audience, singing greetings in several languages and performing greeting actions.

Special people

Musical focus: Beat and tempo   **Area of learning:** Personal, social and emotional development

YELLOW

RESOURCES
Small teddy bear.

TUNE
C C G G
Bounce the teddy

My turn, your turn – teddy

- Show the children a hand-sized cuddly teddy bear and tell them its name, encouraging them to pass the bear from one to another and say hello to it.

- Sit in a circle with the bear in the centre and listen to *My turn, your turn* (*track 3; tune Twinkle twinkle little star*), all tapping knees to the beat, and joining in as the song becomes familiar:

Bounce the ted - dy, fun to do...

Bounce the teddy, fun to do,
Then it's time for someone new.
My turn, your turn, we can share,
My turn, your turn, then it's fair.
Bounce the teddy, fun to do,
Then it's time for someone new.

- Invite one child to take the toy teddy bear. While everyone sings the song and taps their knees to the beat, this child bounces the teddy. At the end of the song the child passes the teddy to the next person in the circle and all sing again.

BLUE

RESOURCES
A collection of cuddly toys from home.

TUNE
C C G G
Stroke the rabbit

TIP
Some children will be able to keep the beat on percussion instruments.

At the end of the song, everyone shakes hands, congratulates and applauds everyone else for the good work they have done.

My turn, your turn – toy parade

- The children each bring a hand-sized cuddly toy from home. Encourage them to share the names of their toys and talk to each other about them.

- Ask the children to make up an action for each toy: stroking the furry rabbit, swinging the monkey, jumping the pony, and so on.

- Invent new verses together for *My turn, your turn*, eg

Stroke the rabbit, fun to do ...

Swing the monkey, fun to do ...

Jump the pony, fun to do ...

- Choose one of the toys and all sing the new verse with or without the CD *(backing track 4)*. One child marks the beat with the toy and its action while the other children copy the movement with their hands.

- When the song is very familiar, pass the toy from one child to the next at the end of each line.

I've got a tambour

- The children sit in a circle with pairs of matching instruments in the centre, eg two tambours, two guiros, two jingles.
- You pick an instrument and invite a child to take the other and be your partner. Everyone chants *I've got a tambour* (*track 5*) while you tap the tambour to the beat:

| I've | got a | tam | -bour. | What | can I | do? |
| I | can | tap | it. | Now | it's | you. |

Everyone repeats the chant as your partner taps the other tambour.

- Continue in this way, choosing a different partner, instrument and playing action each time – but always keeping the beat, eg

I've got jingles. What can I do?
I can shake them. Now it's you.

Kye kye kule

- All sit or stand in a large space. Listen to *Kye kye kule* (*track 6*) and join in with the steady drum beat by tapping part of the body, eg knees, shoulders or chest:

| Kye | kye | ku - le, | Kye | kye | ku - le... |

- All sing the echoes, keeping the beat as before:

Leader:
Kye kye ku - le,
Kye kye kofi nsa,
Kofi nsa langa,
Kaka shi langa,
Kum adende,

Children:
Kye kye ku - le,
Kye kye kofi nsa,
Kofi nsa langa,
Kaka shi langa,
Kum adende.

All: Kum adende. Hey!

- Stand in a circle. Choose one child to go into the circle and keep the beat with a body action while the CD plays or while you lead the singing. The others sing the echoes and copy the action.
- Choose a new leader to perform a different action on the beat as the song is sung again.
- Continue in this way, giving other children the opportunity to lead.

Special people

Musical focus: Beat and tempo   **Area of learning:** Personal, social and emotional development

YELLOW

TIP
Repeat this type of activity frequently, giving the children many opportunities to match movement to sounds performed at regular and changing speeds.

Father and Mother and Uncle Tom

- All listen to *Father and Mother and Uncle Tom* (*track 7*). In a large space say or play the rhyme again, leading the actions and encouraging the children to join in when ready:

Father and Mother and Uncle Tom   *(walk at normal pace as if holding pony's bridle)*
Got on the pony and rode along.
Father fell off,   *(stop and extend hands to one side of body)*
And Mother fell off,   *(extend hands to other side of body)*
And Uncle Tom rode on
   and on and on and on... Whooooa!   *(walk faster and faster until leader calls 'Whooaa')*

- When the leader calls 'Whooaa', everyone stops and remains still until the rhyme starts again.

- Give the children regular practice at speeding up and slowing down their movement in response to sound. You make the sounds and the children match the speed, eg

  - beating an egg (*turn a real egg whisk in a bowl*): the children roll hands round each other;

  - boat (*tap a drum*): the children sit on the floor in facing pairs, holding hands, and make rowing actions;

  - bouncing ball (*bounce a beach ball*): the children jump with feet together.

BLUE

RESOURCES
Ask parents to help make a collection of different kinds of shoes and footwear, eg slippers, wellingtons, trainers, walking shoes, flippers, horse shoes, dancing shoes, etc.

Move in moving shoes

- Listen to *Footwear* (*track 8*) and invite the children to match up the sounds they hear with real footwear from a varied collection. (*Answer: wellingtons, trainers, flippers, walking shoes.*)

- With the children, find action words reflecting a speed which suits the purpose of the footwear:

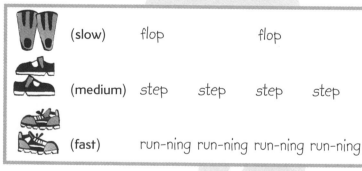

(slow)	flop		flop	
(medium)	step	step	step	step
(fast)	run-ning	run-ning	run-ning	run-ning

- One child puts on shoes from the collection and moves around at an appropriate speed. The others:

  - copy the action with hands or feet at the same speed;

  - say the action words ('swish swish', 'step step') repeatedly in time with the movement.

RESOURCES
Paints and paper.

EXTENSIONS
Some children in pairs, will be able to play instruments on the claps and stamps.

Tape together all the prints of hands and feet making a large quilt. Hang this on the wall and invite the children to make up their own sequences from small sections of the quilt.

Print patterns

- Help the children make prints of their hands and feet on paper. Choose four hand prints and place them in a row in view of everyone.

- The children clap and say 'hand' as you point to each hand print to a steady beat:

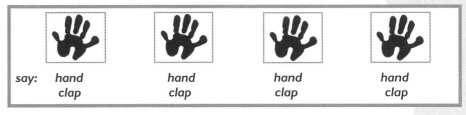

say: *hand clap* *hand clap* *hand clap* *hand clap*

- Do the same with four foot prints:

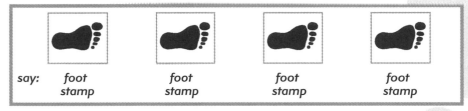

say: *foot stamp* *foot stamp* *foot stamp* *foot stamp*

- Place two hand prints and two foot prints next to each other and perform a sequence of claps and stamps:

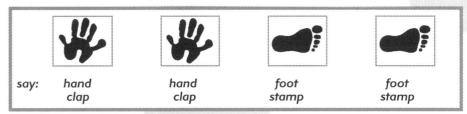

say: *hand clap* *hand clap* *foot stamp* *foot stamp*

- Invite the children to make up a new order, and perform it.

RESOURCES
Full-length mirror.

TUNE
A A A G F♯
If you want to be

EXTENSION
Some children will be able to play instruments at an appropriate speed to accompany the different faces you sing about.

Make a face

- Using a full-length mirror, encourage the children to explore making as many different expressive faces as they can.

- Taking turns, each child makes a body movement to match how they feel when making each face. Help them identify some happy, sad, angry, frightened, sleepy, funny movements. Invite the other children to mirror the lead child's movement.

- Talk about the different speeds of the movements and act them out in front of the mirror.

- Play the song *Make a face* (*track 9*) several times, encouraging the children to join in as it becomes familiar:

If you want to be happy and have a happy day,
And spread a bit of joy around then there is just one way:

Make a face, make a face,
Make it as happy as you can and make a face.

- Make up a new verse for a sad, scared or silly face. Make the new face as you sing at an appropriate speed to match the new mood.

Special people

YELLOW

RESOURCES
A print out of
the story from
the CD-ROM.

Ananse, Puss and Ratta

- Talk about the tricks spiders play, eg making cobwebs on the ceiling, catching flies in webs, startling people by moving quickly across the floor. Tell the children about Ananse spider, a Caribbean story character, who tricks and outwits other animals whenever he can.

- Listen to the story of *Ananse, Puss and Ratta* (track 10).

BLUE

TUNE
   E   G   F
Rat- ta   danced

TIP
Before singing it,
all chant Ratta's
song words,
gradually getting
faster and faster:

Ratta danced
but he could
not stop,
could not stop,
could not stop...
POP!

Ratta's dance

- All dance to *Ratta's dance* (track 11), turning, twisting, bending low, stretching high, and so on. Match the speed of the music, getting faster and faster just like Ratta in the story.

- At 'POP', everyone stops dancing and sits down on the floor.

- Sing the words of *Ratta's dance song* with or without the CD (track 11), gradually getting faster:

Ratta danced but he could not stop, could not stop, could not stop,
Ratta danced but he could not stop, could not stop, could not stop...

Spider tricks

GREEN

RESOURCES
A range of untuned percussion instruments.

EXTENSION
Three children, each with an instrument you have explored, sit out of sight of the others. Point to one child who plays one of the action sounds. The other children respond with the matching movement.

Little Miss Muffet

- Say *Little Miss Muffet* (*reference track 12*) with hand actions, repeating it until the children can join in with you confidently:

Little Miss Muffet sat on her tuffet, *(medium-paced bowl to mouth movement)*
Eating her curds and whey.
There came a big spider, *(slow, creeping hand movement)*
Who sat down beside her
And frightened Miss Muffet away. *(fingers running quickly away)*

- Draw attention to the changes in the speed of each action and ask three children to choose and play an instrument to match, eg

  – spoon action: rainmaker tipped steadily side to side;
  – creeping: guiro scraped slowly;
  – running: tambourine shaken quickly

- Say the rhyme with the actions, while three children accompany with the chosen instrumental sounds on the appropriate lines.

GREY

RESOURCES
A range of untuned percussion instruments.

Ananse card: photocopy and cut out the Ananse illustration on this page.

EXTENSION
Explore combinations of vocal, body and instrumental sounds for each of Ananse's actions.

Brer Ananse Spider

- Talk with the children about spider movements, eg a quick stop and start scamper when in danger, busy web spinning, dropping quickly down a strand of silk, staying very still.

- Using vocal sounds, body percussion or instruments, encourage the children to create sounds to match the movements discussed, eg

  – scampering stop-start run: vocal 'ticka ticka ticka', tap fingertips on a hard surface, scrape a guiro;

  – slow web spinning: rub palms together continuously, flick tambourine jingles quietly and continuously;

  – dropping down on a silken thread: vocal high to low 'weeee'; tap a chime bar once.

- Familiarise the children with *Brer Ananse Spider* (*track 19*):

Brer Ananse Spider,
What tricks will you play?

If you do not harm me,
I will...

...stay and play. *(happy medium-paced sounds)*
...sleep all day. *(gentle slow sounds)*
...run away. *(light and fast sounds)*

- The children sit in a circle and pass round an Ananse card as they say the chant. At the words, 'If you do not harm me, I will...', the child holding the card completes the rhyme with one of the three endings. The child sitting next in the circle performs a vocal, body percussion or instrumental sound to match Ananse's action.

Special people

Musical focus: Beat and tempo   **Area of learning:** Personal, social and emotional development

YELLOW

TIP
Ask parents to guide children in observing birds, and how they use their wings to fly

Bird melodies

- The children listen to the melody of *Baak bakum paira* (*track 14*) played quickly, and sway their bodies to the fast beat of the music, moving their arms quickly like the wings of a small bird, such as a dove.

- The children listen to the melody of *Baak bakum paira* (*track 15*) played slowly, and respond to the slower speed by stretching their bodies and moving their hands and arms more slowly and strongly like the wings of a bigger bird, such as a swan.

BLUE

TUNE
F D G E C
Bye baby bunting

Bye baby bunting

- Listen to *Bye baby bunting* (*track 16*) and explain the story behind the song: a baby sleeps while his father goes hunting and his mother finds a soft, warm fur to keep the baby warm.

- Explain that some dancers tell stories using body movements. Sing *Bye baby bunting* (*track 16*), finding dance hand movements to illustrate each line, eg

Bye baby bunting,	*(side of head lying on closed hands)*
Daddy's gone a hunting,	*(hand to brow, searching)*
Mummy's gone to fetch a skin	*(stroke fur slowly and gently)*
To wrap the baby bunting in.	*(rock baby in arms)*

- Sing the song with the actions several times, getting slower each time until 'the baby' falls asleep.

GREEN

RESOURCES
a print out of the story from the CD-ROM.

TUNE
F F Eb D
Baak bakum

BACKGROUND
The Bengali words mean:

*Coo, dove,
Bring the wedding crown.
The bride marries tomorrow,
She will go away in a golden palenquin.*

The magic dove

- Explain that in Bengali the words 'baak bakum' are like the sound the dove makes when it coos. Tell the story, *The magic dove*, or play the CD recording of it (*track 17, text on CD-ROM*). At the end of the story, all join in with the actions for the song:

Baak bakum paira,   *(link thumbs and move fingers like bird wings)*

Matay die taira,   *(make crown with upstretched fingers and place on head)*

Bow shazbe kalki,   *(place palms together and move them in a circle for wedding)*

Chorrbe shonaar palki.   *(step hands in front of each other)*

Baak bakum paira 🔊

- Sing or play the recording of *Baak bakum paira* (*track 18*) several times, encouraging the children to join in as it becomes familiar.

- Tell *The magic dove* story, encouraging the children's participation:

    – joining in with the rhymes;

    – performing the song with the dance hand movements;

    – acting out the events (*small group*).

- Share a performance with parents and other children.

GREY

TIP
Play the melody of *Baak bakum paira* (*track 14*) before and after the performance to set the atmosphere of the story.

Special people

Musical focus: Beat and tempo **Area of learning:** Personal, social and emotional development

RESOURCES
Make large copies of the Chinese characters on the CD-ROM to decorate the setting.

TUNE
A B C♯ E
Chinese New Year

BACKGROUND
春節 Chunjié -
New Year

Chinese New Year – first verse

- Ask parents to talk with their children about celebrating special occasions. Together, talk about Chinese New Year and things associated with its celebration, eg lanterns, bright costumes, packets of money, fireworks and special food.

- Encourage the children to tap knees and sway to the beat as they listen to the first verse of *Chinese New Year* (track 19).

Chi-nese New Year   is here   a - gain,   here   a -gain...

- Listen to *Chinese New Year* again, encouraging the children to join in as it becomes familiar.

Chinese New Year is here again, here again, here again,
Chinese New Year is here again – chunjié, chunjié, chunjié.

TIP
Encourage the children to vary the speed of their movements each time they repeat the chant.

A dragon moves like this

- Show the children the videoclip of the Chinese New Year celebrations in Soho, London. Talk about the way in which the dancers move.

- Discuss how an imaginary dragon might arch, run, slide, sway, shuffle, weave, pounce, pause, and so on.

- Ask the children to talk about and imitate the ways their pets move.

- In a large space, use this chant to explore the movements you have discussed:

> My (cat), (name of pet) –
>   moves like this, *(say the words quietly while imitating the pet's movement)*
> But a dragon –
>   moves like this. *(say the words loudly while imitating the dragon's movement)*

- All join in singing the first verse of *Chinese New Year* (track 19), while moving individually like the imaginary dragons.

GREEN

TUNE
A B C♯ E
Chinese New Year

BACKGROUND
The Chinese words mean:

龍 lung – dragon

爆竹 baozhu – firecracker

錢 qian – money

舞 wu – dance

TIP
Spend some time becoming familiar with the song yourself before playing it to the children.

Ask parents to contribute to a collection of festive items: lights and lanterns, party poppers, blowers and hats, etc.

GREY

RESOURCES
Lengths of colourful cloth.

A range of instruments.

TIP
Make the final performance colourful with masks, bright costumes, lanterns and streamers.

EXTENSION
Some children may be able to form a longer dragon by joining hands and moving together.

Chinese New Year – complete

- Listen to the whole song, *Chinese New Year* (track 20), and compare the Chinese celebrations with those that the children have experienced at home. Join in singing all the verses:

Chinese New Year is here again, here again, here again,
Chinese New Year is here again – chunjié, chunjié, chunjié.

Look at the dragon breathing flames...
    – lung, lung, lung.

Crackers are banging in the street...
    – baozhu, baozhu, baozhu.

Children have packets of money to spend...
    – qian, qian, qian.

Everyone dances through the streets...
    – wu, wu, wu.

- Explore vocal sounds, body percussion and instruments to accompany the instrumental repeat of each verse on track 20, eg

    – flames: vocal 'wooosh', cymbals clashed together;
    – fireworks: sticks tapped together;
    – money: tambourine jingles tapped lightly.

- All sing the song while some of the children play their sounds during the instrumental repeat of each verse (*track 20*).

Dragon swoops

- Everyone sits in a wide circle. Listen to *Dragon swoops* (track 21), noticing the changes in speed of the dragon's movements:

Dragon swoops and swallows the sea,
Then glides with the clouds – powerful, free.
On scorched earth below, sun-cracked and dry,
Golden dragon tears fall from the sky.

- Invite individual children to enter the circle and explore and refine movements at different speeds, eg gliding, swooping, running, sliding, weaving, shuffling, pouncing, pausing, and so on. Give each child a length of flowing, silky material to hold over their backs as they move. Give several children turns to be dragons.

- Select two or three children to be dragons as you say the poem or play the recording (*track 21*).

- Notice the sounds which accompany the recording. Explore instruments to accompany your own performance, pairing up players and dragons.

- While a small group of children move as dragons, their partners accompany them, responding to the speed of their movements with their chosen instruments.

Going places

Musical focus: High and low   **Area of learning:** Communication, language and literacy

YELLOW

RESOURCES
a print out of the rap from the CD-ROM.

TIP

Act out the rhyme. You play Mr Noah, sitting in the middle of a circle. Divide the children into animal groups, and invite them into your 'ark' in the centre, making their animal sounds and actions as they join you.

Please, Mr Noah – part one

- Listen to *Please, Mr Noah*, part one (*track 22, text on CD-ROM*):

- Encourage the children to join in with the actions for each animal, and with high- and low-pitched vocal sounds after each verse:

mice (high-pitched):

Squeak squeak squeak squeak,
Squeak squeak squeak squeak.

lions (low-pitched):

Roar_____ roar,_____
Roar_____ roar._____

monkeys (high-pitched):

Chitter chatter chitter chatter,
Chitter chatter chitter chatter.

bears (low-pitched):

Growl_____ growl,_____
Growl_____ growl._____

BLUE

TIP
Invite one of the children to lead the game.

Animal antics

- Encourage the children to explore whole body movements for mice, lions, monkeys and bears, eg:

  - mice: quick, scampering movements;

  - lions: walk on all fours, with head held proudly;

  - monkeys: move on feet with arms above heads as if swinging from branch to branch;

  - bears: walking slowly with heavy feet.

- Play *Animal antics*. Whenever you squeak or chatter, roar or growl in a high or low voice respectively, the children respond quickly with the appropriate animal movement.

GREEN

RESOURCES
A print out of the rap from the CD-ROM.

TIP
Encourage the children to say each animal's sound words distinctly, making clear differences between high and low in their voices.

Please, Mr Noah – complete

- Listen to *Please, Mr Noah* parts one and two (*tracks 22-23*), performing the actions and joining in with the animal sound words:

Squeak squeak squeak squeak.

Roar_____ roar._____

Chitter chatter chitter chatter.

Growl_____ growl._____

- Perform the rap without the CD.

GREY

TIP
Simple mask templates, which may be printed out and coloured in by the children are provided on the CD-ROM to enhance the performance. Attach the coloured animal face to a circlet of card and remember to cut out eye holes as positioned.

Launch the ark

- Sit in a circle with a selection of instruments and soundmakers in the centre.

- Ask a child to choose an instrument for one of the animals in *Please, Mr Noah*, eg finger cymbals for the mice. Ask the child to play as the others repeat the words 'squeak, squeak, squeak':

Squeak   squeak   squeak   squeak

- Decide with the group whether the choice and manner of playing is appropriate, eg does it give a clear sense of high pitch?

- Ask three other children each to choose instrumental sounds for the lions, monkeys and bears. Discuss and refine the choices together by playing and saying the animal sound words together.

- Give small groups of children practice at adding the chosen instrumental sounds to the rap as the other children perform it.

- Give a grand performance of *Please, Mr Noah* with:

  – rappers, who perform the rap;

  – movers, who make whole body animal movements and enact the story with one child playing the part of Mr Noah, while the others enter the ark as animals;

  – instrument players, who provide the animal sounds.

Going places

Musical focus: High and low   **Area of learning:** Communication, language and literacy

Three bears' rap

- Tell the story of *Goldilocks and the Three Bears* in your own words or from a favourite published version.

- Listen to *Three bears' rap* (track 24, text on CD-ROM). Encourage the children to copy you as you show the different pitches of the three bears' growls with these actions:

    – tapping your knees as you make low growls (*Papa Bear*);

    – tapping your shoulders as you make medium growls (*Mama Bear*);

    – lifting hands in the air as you make high growls (*Wee Bear*).

- Listen to the CD again and encourage the children to join in with the low-, medium- and high-pitched bear voices and with the low, medium and high actions.

- As the rhyme becomes familiar, add more actions, eg eating porridge, rocking back and forth in a rocking chair, and lying curled up in a bed.

Bear talk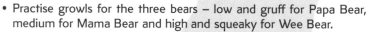

- Practise growls for the three bears – low and gruff for Papa Bear, medium for Mama Bear and high and squeaky for Wee Bear.

- Hold up the bear cards one at a time and encourage the children to make each bear's growly voice at the appropriate pitch.

- Listen to *Three bears' rap* (*track 24*) and join in with the bears' growls, displaying the appropriate card as its bear is mentioned.

The Three Bears

GREEN

RESOURCES
Cards of the three bears' heads (see page 22).

A small box or bag in which to place the cards during this passing game.

TIP
Make your growls very distinctive!

Let a child perform the growl at the end of the chant.

Prowl and growl

- Sit in a circle. Show the children the three bears' cards and make sure that they can identify each one by name.

- Practise the three growls at their appropriate pitches: low and gruff for Papa Bear, medium for Mama Bear and high and squeaky for Wee Bear.

- Put the cards into a box or bag and pass it round the circle while you say this chant:

Bears in the wood,
Out on the prowl!
Which bear's speaking?
Listen to the growl!

At the end of the chant, ask the children to listen to your 'growl'. The child holding the box selects the correct bear picture and holds it up.

- Play the game again.

GREY

TIP
The association of low, medium and high voices with the low, medium and high actions helps the children to 'feel' the pitch.

Bear show

- Listen to *Three bears' rap* (*track 24*), joining in with the growls and marking the three pitches with the hand positions described in YELLOW level.

- Encourage the children to join in with the repeated lines: 'said the Papa Bear', 'said the Mama Bear' and 'said the Wee Bear' and the final 'Don't you dare!'. As the rhyme becomes more familiar, the children will be able to join in with all of it.

- Perform the rap without the CD to parents or another group. Make sure that the pitch of your voice matches the pitch of the three bears' voices and encourage everyone to join in as much of the rap as they can and with growls and matching hand actions.

Going places

Musical focus: High and low   Area of learning: Communication, language and literacy

YELLOW

VIDEOCLIPS
Reference clips of these YELLOW, BLUE, GREEN and GREY activities are included on the CD-ROM.

RESOURCES
A Jack-in-the-box toy if available.

TUNE
G G G E
Jack lives in a

Jack-in-the-box

• Talk with the children about their favourite toys. Show the children a real Jack-in-the box or the videoclip on the CD–ROM (c2).

• Listen to the song *Jack-in-the-box* (*track 25*), and encourage the children to place their hands on their heads for the lid of the box, press their noses on the word 'button' and fling their arms up on 'pops', reaching high when they hear the high note.

Jack lives in a wooden box,
Head squashed down between his socks.
Press the button and up he pops!
My Jack-in-the-box!

Jack lives under a wooden lid,
No one knows just where he hid,
Press the button and up he pops!
My Jack-in-the-box!

Jack lives in a house of wood,
He's a toy that's always good,
Press the button and up he pops!
My Jack-in-the-box!

BLUE

TUNE
G G G E
Jack lives in a

TIP
Help the children get into a curled up position from which they can leap (*some will want to lie flat rather than crouch*). Start by standing up with hands on head, and gradually sink into a crouch keeping feet flat on the floor.

Jack jump high, Jack hide low

• Listen to *Jack-in-the-box* (*track 25*) and sing along with the chorus:

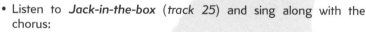

Press the button and up he pops!
My Jack-in-the-box!

• Encourage the children to press their noses for the 'button' and fling their arms into the air for 'pops'.

• Ask the children to curl up into small shapes like Jack in his box. When you call 'Jack jump HIGH' encourage them to jump up tall with their arms high in the air. When you call 'Jack hide LOW' they shrink back down to their curled up shapes.

• In a large space, sing Jack-in-the-box with or without the CD and use these high and low whole body movements: jumping up high on 'Up he pops' and sinking down low on 'My Jack-in-the-box'.

GREEN

RESOURCES
a print out of the story from the CD-ROM.

TUNE
G G G E
Jack lives in a

TIP
A flexitone, played by an adult, makes a wonderful 'wibble wobble' sound to accompany the first chant.

A swanee whistle or glockenspiel played from highest-sounding to lowest-sounding bars might accompany the second chant.

The Jack factory

- Sing *Jack-in-the-box* (*track 25*) and use whole body actions for popping up and sinking down.

- Listen to *The Jack Factory* story (*track 26, text on CD-ROM*).

- After hearing the story, say the Jack chants on their own, inviting the children to join in on 'zing zing zing' and 'flip, flip, flip':

Zing zing zing,
My head's on a spring,
Wibble wobble, wibble wobble,
Zing zing zing.

Hip flip flip,
Down I slip,
Squashed inside my little box,
Clunk goes the clip.

- Move to a large space inside or outside. Say the chant, *Zing zing zing*, and ask the children to stand on the spot and wobble from side to side, jiggling their heads.

- Now say the chant, *Flip flip flip*, and ask the children to tap their hands on their heads as they gradually sink into a crouched shape.

- Divide the children into two groups with one group joining in with the words of the chant, and the other performing the actions.

GREY

RESOURCES
Paint 'Jack' faces on paper plates and fix them to sticks.

Drape a sheet over two chairs to make a puppet screen.

A selection of instruments and soundmakers.

TUNE

G E F
We're Jacks and

TIP
Place a Jack paper plate and instruments in the music corner where the children can use them to tell Jack's story.

The Jack factory puppet show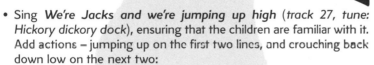

- Sing *We're Jacks and we're jumping up high* (*track 27, tune: Hickory dickory dock*), ensuring that the children are familiar with it. Add actions – jumping up on the first two lines, and crouching back down low on the next two:

We're Jacks and we're jumping up high,
Our heads are all touching the sky,
We won't stay down when we go to town,
We're lonely and starting to cry.

- Prepare a puppet show in which:

  - some children manipulate paper plate Jack puppets behind a screen, popping them up or down in response to the story;

  - some children choose and perform sounds for the wobbly springy movements, while others make lid 'flip' sounds to accompany the chants;

  - everyone else performs the actions, chants and song while you tell or play the CD of *The Jack Factory*.

Going places

Musical focus: High and low   **Area of learning:** Communication, language and literacy

YELLOW

TUNE
G C' G G
Hands high look at

Sky-high, toe-low

• Listen to *Sky-high, toe-low* (track 28):

Hands high, look at me,
To the sky, look at me,
Hands low, look at me,
To my toes, look at me.
Now I stand with my hands in the air.

Hands high, look at me,
To the sky, look at me,
Hands low, look at me,
To my toes, look at me.
Now I stand with my hands way down there.

• Sing the song and model the hand actions for the children:

– on 'high', 'sky', 'air' raise hands above head;

– on 'low', 'toes', 'there' drop hands down low;

– on all other words bring your hands to your middle.

• Invite the children to join in with the song and the high, low and middle actions where they can.

• Tell the children that this time when you sing the song, the ending will be a surprise – they need to listen carefully to hear which action to perform: high hands or low hands. Sing one of the verses. Did the children respond correctly? Repeat until all can confidently and correctly respond to the high or low ending.

BLUE

TUNE
G C' G G
Jumping high look

TIP
Make the actions as high and low as possible to show a real contrast.

Jumping high

• Listen to *Jumping high* (track 29) and model the whole body actions suggested by the song: jump on 'high' and 'sky'; crouch down on 'low' and 'toes'. As before raise or lower hands on the last line.

Jumping high, look at me,
To the sky, look at me,
Crouching low, look at me,
To my toes, look at me.
Now I stand with my hands in the air.

Jumping high, look at me...
Now I stand with my hands way down there.

• Divide the class into two groups. One group performs the actions while the other sings the verses in a previously agreed order.

GREEN

RESOURCES
Alto xylophone with low C, middle G and high C' bars.

TIP
Let a child play the high and low notes. Some children may be able to respond with their backs to the player, so that the children rely solely on their listening skills.

EXTENSION
Add the middle G bar between the high C and low C bars. The children put their hands in a middle position when they hear it played.

GREY

TUNE
D D D D
Fish in the blue

TIP
Make a set of fish-bird hand puppets from the templates on the CD-ROM, attaching one fish and one bird picture back to back. Give every child one to hold. Stand up and sing the song holding the puppets high and low on the appropriate lines.

High, low, do you know?

- Sing *Sky-high, toe-low* (*track 28*) with the actions.

- Show the children a xylophone with all the bars removed except the low C bar (longer) and the high C bar (shorter). Play these two notes several times to familiarise the children with the difference between the high and low sounds.

- Ask the children to respond when they hear the high note by putting their hands high in the air.

- Ask them to crouch down low when they hear the low note.

Fish swim – birds fly

- Sing *Sky-high, toe-low* without the CD and perform the actions.

- Listen to the song *Fish in the blue sea* (*track 30*) and join in.

Fish in the blue sea,
Birds in the sky.
Fish swim below and
Birds fly high!

- Talk with the children about swimming and flying and the parts of birds' and fishes' bodies that help them to make these movements. Encourage them to use their arms to invent actions. Try these out while you sing.

- Now practise the swimming action with hands near the floor to reinforce the 'low' notes and flying hand actions, high in the air to match the high notes.

Going places

Musical focus: High and low   **Area of learning:** Communication, language and literacy

YELLOW

RESOURCES
Candles.
Mouse finger puppets (*make them from the fingers of old gloves*). Make at least one for yourself, and if possible one for each child.

TUNE
C C C C
Up the tall white

TIP
Use this song as an opportunity to talk with the children about the dangers of candles and live flames.

Little Mousie Brown

- Show the children some candles, including one tall one.

- Talk about occasions when we light candles – birthdays, Christmas, Hannukah, Diwali, power cuts...

- Show the children a mouse finger puppet and give one to each child if available.

- Listen to *Little Mousie Brown* (*track 31*) and let your finger puppet move up the candle, using the whole song to reach the top then let your finger puppet move quickly down again with the music.

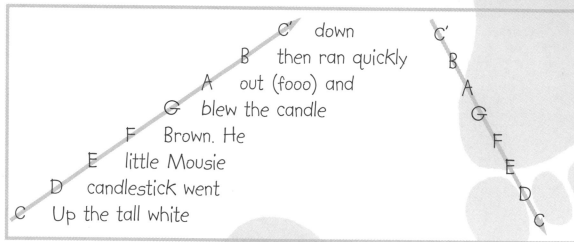

- Listen again and invite the children to mime the action. Bend one arm at the elbow so that the fingertips point up. This is the candle and the wiggling fingers become the dancing flame. One finger (*or finger puppet*) on the other hand is Mousie Brown who inches slowly up the other arm. When he blows out the flame, the children blow on their wiggling fingers and then clench them in a fist as the flame goes out. Let 'Mousie Brown' climb down the arm again.

BLUE

RESOURCES
Xylophone with notes:
C D E F G A B C'

TIP
Play the tune and hand pattern from high to low as well as low to high. Play the tune on other pitched instruments such as a recorder, glockenspiel or keyboard.

Mousie Brown goes up and down

- Listen to *Little Mousie Brown* (*track 31*) and sing along with the CD, including the mimed actions.

- Use a xylophone to play a slow eight-note tune, starting on the long, low C bar. You will end on the short, high C' bar (*reference track 32*).

- Talk with the children about how the notes 'step' up. This is explained more easily if you up-end the xylophone like a ladder with the longest note at the bottom.

- Play the eight-note xylophone tune and ask another adult to model a hand stepping pattern by letting one hand move from the floor to chin in eight 'steps'. Invite the children to copy. Practise several times.

- Try this hand pattern while you sing *Little Mousie Brown*.

Mousie Brown

GREEN

RESOURCES
Xylophone with notes:
C D E F G A B C'

TIP
Some children will be able to play the *Candle creepers* tune on xylophone to lead the others' actions.

Candle creepers

- Listen to *Little Mousie Brown* (*track 31*) and sing it with hand actions with or without the CD.

- Listen to *Candle creepers* (*track 33*) and use hand 'steps' to mark the tune stepping up and down.

- Find a space and crouch down into a small shape. Listen to *Candle creepers* and gradually straighten up into a tall stretched shape as the rising tune is played and sink down again for the falling tune.

- Arrange the children into pairs. Explain that one of each pair is the tall, straight candle. The partner is going to be 'Mousie Brown'.

  The 'candles' stand strong and tall. The 'mice' start crouched behind their 'candles' and as the *Candle creepers* tune plays, they walk their hands up their partner from feet upwards, straightening up to reach the top of the candle. As the music gets lower, the 'mice' walk their hands back down their partners.

- Swap roles and play again.

- Play the activity outdoors using a xylophone to play the *Candle creepers* tune.

GREY

TIP
Some children may be able to build 'fist towers' in pairs: each partner adds in alternate fists.

Mousie Brown counts

- Sing *Little Mousie Brown* (*track 31*) with actions.

- Listen to *Mousie Brown counts* (*track 34*).

- Sing the numbers from one to eight along with Mousie Brown as you listen to the song.

- Now practise building a fist tower while you sing the numbers from one to eight in *Mousie Brown counts*. Sit down and place one fist on your knee as you sing 'one'. Place your other fist on top of the first as you sing 'two'. Take the lower fist away and place it on top of the other when you sing 'three'. Keep building your tower until you reach number eight. Your tower will probably reach your chin!

- When everyone is familiar with this activity, organise half the class to build fist towers while the other half sing *Little Mousie Brown*. Swap over and perform again.

Musical focus: High and low   **Area of learning:** Communication, language and literacy

---

YELLOW

RESOURCES
Make or bring in some popcorn.

Make popcorn shakers with cooked and uncooked popcorn in plastic transparent jars.

TUNE
C' C C' C
Popcorn, popcorn

TIP
Use small amounts of popcorn in each shaker to allow lots of sound and movement. Try one shaker with uncooked corn and one with cooked popcorn. Can the children hear any difference in the sound?

Popcorn – part one

- Listen to the first part of *Popcorn* (*track 35*), clapping on the syllables 'pop' and 'corn'

Part one

Popcorn, popcorn,
Popping out of the pan.
Popcorn popcorn,
Eat as much as you can!

- Talk with the children about popcorn. Have any of their parents made it for them? Bring in some sweet and salted popcorn to try or make some in your setting.

- Make shakers with transparent plastic screw top jars containing popcorn. Use these to accompany the song, shaking instead of clapping on the words 'popcorn'.

BLUE

RESOURCES
A swanee whistle.

TIP
If no whistle is available use your own voice or play a xylophone, sliding the beater up and down the bars.

Poppers

- Show the children a swanee whistle and see if they can tell you what happens to the sound when the plunger is pushed in and then pulled out (*it rises to a high note, falls to a low note*).

- Ask them to make low shapes near the ground. When they hear the swanee whistle playing a fast low to high slide (*starting with the plunger out*) they should suddenly spring up like popcorn when it is cooked, and stand tall. (*Make the upwards slide quick to suggest the speedy jump of a cooked grain of corn bursting up.*)

- When the whistle plays the opposite slide, falling back to a low note, the children should sink down again. (*The sinking slide can be much slower and more evenly played.*)

Popcorn

GREEN

RESOURCES
A variety of instruments and soundmakers.

TIP
A child might conduct the 'pop' music interlude. Hold up an open hand for 'play' and a closed fist for 'stop'. Alternatively use a 'stop/go' green and red lollipop.

Pop music

- Listen to *Popcorn* (*track 35*), clapping on the syllables 'pop' and 'corn' but encouraging the children to clap above their heads on 'pop' and by their knees on 'corn', to match the high and low notes.

- Sit in a circle with a selection of instruments and soundmakers in the centre. Ask a few children to choose instruments that will make 'popping' sounds, such as woodblocks, sticks, drums and tambours or plastic bubble wrap.

- Sing the song again with popping sounds on the syllables 'pop' and 'corn' only.

- Create a 'pop' music interlude and play it between repeats of the song.

  Every child chooses an instrument or soundmaker from the centre. You are the conductor. Stand with your arms stretched above your head, palms touching. The music begins as you move one arm round in a complete circle like a hand on a clock face. When your two hands touch again the music stops.

GREY

RESOURCES
A variety of instruments and soundmakers.

Xylophone or chime bar notes: low C and high C.

TUNE
A   A   A   B
Eat it   at the

Popcorn – complete

- Listen to the complete song, *Popcorn* (*track 36*), encouraging the children to rock imaginary popcorn bags from side to side on their knees in the new part of the song.

Part one
Popcorn, popcorn...

Part two
Eat it at the cinema,
Balanced on your knee.
Will it last you 'til the end?
You will have to wait and see!

Part one (repeat)
Popcorn, popcorn...

- Ask a few children to play 'popping sounds' for the syllables 'pop' and 'corn' on instruments or soundmakers.

- Play alternate high and low C on chime bars or on a xylophone on 'pop' and 'corn' and encourage everyone else to clap above their heads and then by their knees to mark the high and low notes. Try singing without the CD.

- Play an interlude of improvised 'popping' music, conducted as in GREEN level, then sing and accompany the whole song again.

Moving patterns

Musical focus: Structure   **Area of learning:** Mathematical development

Pass the pebble on the beat

- Sit in a circle and listen to the song *Pass the pebble on* (track 37). Pat your knees in time to the fast beat (*the higher-sounding steady beat on the recording*) and encourage the children to copy you:

Pass the peb - ble on.   Try to keep it stea-dy ...

- Repeat the song many times, tapping the beat on other parts of the body or on the floor.

Who has the pebble? – chant

- Sit in a circle and place one coloured pebble in front of three children.

- Model this chant by saying each question and answer very rhythmically:

Who has the *blue* pebble?
Ginnie has the *blue* pebble.

Who has the *red* pebble?
Daniel has the *red* pebble.

Who has the *yellow* pebble...

- Play again and encourage the children to join in with the answers.

- When the question and answer pattern is established, finish with:

How many altogether?
There are three.

Pebbles

GREEN

RESOURCES
Five coloured pebbles.
A tambour.

TUNE
G E A G
Who has the blue

TIP
You may find that a child is able to lead by singing the questions, but continue to support the activity by maintaining the beat.

Who has the pebble? – song

* Sit in a circle. Place one coloured pebble in front of five children.

* Model the sung question and answer pattern yourself (*reference track 38*):

Who has the *blue* pebble?
Alice has the *blue* pebble.

* Encourage the children to join in with the answers using the appropriate names.

* Keep a strong pulse throughout this activity by tapping your knee or playing a clear beat on a tambour.

GREY

RESOURCES
One pebble or beanbag.

TUNE
G E G E
Pass the peb – ble

EXTENSION
With practice and familiarity, the children will develop the skill to play the game themselves, passing the pebble on the beat while singing the song. The objective is to pass the pebble without missing a beat or dropping the pebble.

Pass the pebble on

* Show the children the videoclip of the game, *Pass the pebble on* (*P 12*). Notice how the children pass the pebble on to the slow, steady beat (*played by a low-sounding drum on the recording*).

* Sit in a circle and listen to the song *Pass the pebble on* (*track 37*) joining in with the words when they are familiar:

Pass the pebble on, try to keep it steady.
Pass the pebble on, try to keep it steady.

You'll soon be out if you don't keep in time with the beat.
You'll soon be out if you don't keep in time with the beat.

* Begin teaching the game by passing a pebble round the ring yourself. You sit inside the circle. Move the pebble on the slow beat, tapping the floor in front of every child as you turn. Sing the song with the support of the CD:

Pass the peb - ble on.   Try to keep it stea -dy ...

* Encourage the children to clap on the beat when the pebble taps on the floor.

* When this is established, perform the song without the CD. Encourage the children to sing the song and clap the beat while you pass the pebble round the ring.

Moving patterns

Musical focus: Structure **Area of learning:** Mathematical development

YELLOW

TUNE
G D G
All a – lone

Dee-di-diddle-o

- Sit in a circle holding hands. Listen to *Dee-di-diddle-o* (*track 39*) and encourage everyone to swing joined arms freely to the music:

All alone, sitting on the floor,
Dee-di-diddle-o, here's one more.

Two fine friends, sitting on the floor,
Dee-di-diddle-o, here's one more.

Three fine friends ...

Four fine friends ...

Five fine friends, sitting on the floor,
We have five and we don't need more.

- Play the song again, but this time one child sits in the middle of the circle. After listening to verse one, stop the CD and ask this child to choose a friend to join him or her in the centre.

- Sing verse two with the CD. Stop the music again and ask the second child to choose a friend to go into the middle.

- Repeat with all five verses, inviting the children to join in with the singing where they can.

BLUE

RESOURCES
Paper slips of the children's names and a box.

TIP
Practise making the repeated 'd' sounds in 'Dee-di-diddle-o' really clear.

Round we go!

- Put paper slips each bearing a child's name into a box.

- All stand in a circle. Pick out a name from the box and ask that child to stand in the centre.

- All join hands. Sing *Dee-di-diddle-o* without the CD, walking round the child in the centre. At the end of each verse, dip into the box to identify the next child. Encourage the growing group in the centre to join hands and walk round in an inner circle.

- As the game becomes familiar, ask different children to 'dip' for names.

GREEN

TIP
Play a steady beat on a drum or tambour to keep the chant rhythmical.

EXTENSION
Optional verse:

Darren's in the
  middle,
Darren's
  number one,
Darren leaves
  the middle,
And that leaves
  none.

Friends in the middle

- Choose five 'friends' to sit in the middle of the circle. Help the children to count to five out loud as you indicate each child.

- Say the first verse of the chant substituting one of the five children's names for Jaspar on line three. The selected child joins the outer circle, leaving four in the centre:

Friends in the middle,
Friends on the floor,
Jaspar leaves the middle,
And that leaves four.

- Continue with the rest of the chant, counting the number of children in the centre after each verse:

Friends in the middle,
Friends you can see,
Kirsty leaves the middle,
And that leaves three.

Friends in the middle,
Friends like me and you,
Rajit leaves the middle,
And that leaves two!

Friends in the middle,
Friends make it fun,
Darren leaves the middle,
And that leaves one!

- Play the game again, encouraging the children to say the final line of each verse with you.

Add a sound 🔊 39))

GREY

RESOURCES
Five different instruments or soundmakers, eg tambour, woodblock, cymbal, chime bar, metal spoons.

- Ensure that the children can sing *Dee-di-diddle-o* (*track 39*) confidently with you.

- Place five instruments or soundmakers in the centre and ask a child to enter the circle and choose one of the instruments. This child plays freely during the first verse as the others sing it.

- Each new verse is accompanied by an extra child who is invited to select one of the remaining instruments and to join in playing freely.

  Continue until all five instruments are being played together by the five children in the middle.

- Repeat the activity with a new child in the middle.

Moving patterns

Musical focus: Structure   Area of learning: Mathematical development

The missing dumplings

- Talk with the children about the picture on the CD-ROM of a Caribbean market, showing stalls and foods.

- Ask parents if they can contribute souvenirs, photos or products from these islands.

- Hold a Caribbean food day with a fruit salad of exotic, tropical fruits for the children to try.

- Listen to the story of *The missing dumplings* (*track 40*).

Dumplings – song

- Talk with the children about dumplings and make some with help from parents.

- Listen to the song, *Dumplings* (*track 41*).

- Encourage the children to join in with Jamie's responses.

Call:

Jamie, you see nobody pass here?
Jamie, you see nobody pass here?
Well, one of me dumplings gone,
One of me dumplings gone!

Jamie, you see nobody pass here?
Well, two of me dumplings gone ...

Jamie, you see nobody pass here?
Well, three of me dumplings gone ...

Response:

No, me friend.
No, me friend.
Don't tell me so!

No, me friend...

No, me friend...

Dumplings

GREEN

RESOURCES
A plate.
Four beanbags.

TIP
Buy or make some real dumplings for the children.

Four fat dumplings

- The children sit in as wide a circle as possible with a plate of four beanbags in the middle.

- Explain to the children that the beanbags represent four dumplings, which the cook has just taken out of the pot. They are too hot so they have to cool down before they can be eaten.

- Tell the children that they are the 'crows' who want to steal the delicious dumplings.

- You sit in the middle of the circle being the sleeping cook. Say the chant, *Four fat dumplings* (*reference track 42*) together:

Four fat dumplings in de Dutch pot,
Tek them out quickly them hot hot hot,
We have to cool them down in the hall hall hall,
I jus hope the crows don't thief them all.

When the chant ends the 'crows' move very quietly towards the dumplings. If you hear any sound at all, you wake up and chase the birds away by flapping your hands.

- Can the 'crows' move so quietly that they reach the dumplings? If a 'crow' is successful, start the game again with three dumplings.

GREY

RESOURCES
Access to a computer to show the CD-ROM picture of a Caribbean market, or a colour print out.

TUNE
F♯ A A A
Ja –mie, you see

Dumpling swap

- All sing *Dumplings* with or without the CD, performing both parts: the cook's call, 'Jamie, you see nobody pass here?' and Jamie's response, 'No, me friend.' Ensure that the song is secure.

- Look carefully at the picture of the Caribbean market and name as many foods as possible, eg bananas, mangos, fish, breadfruit, etc. Devise new verses together using the names of the foods you have observed.

- Divide the children into two groups, one to sing the cook's call, and the other to sing Jamie's response. Ask another practitioner to lead one of the groups while you lead the other. Sing your new verses:

Call	*Response*
Jamie, you see nobody pass here?	No, me friend.
Jamie, you see nobody pass here?	No, me friend.
Well, one of me mangos gone,	Don't tell me so!
One of me mangos gone!	

Moving patterns

Musical focus: Structure   **Area of learning:** Mathematical development

YELLOW

TUNE
A   B A G
Stamp your feet and

Stamp and clap

- Stand in a circle and listen to the first verse of *Stamp and clap* (*track 43, tune: Polly put the kettle on*). Encourage the children to join in by stamping every time they hear 'stamp' and by clapping on every 'clap', just as on the CD:

Stamp your feet and clap your hands,
Stamp your feet and clap your hands,
Stamp your feet and clap your hands,
We'll stamp and clap.

- Sing again with or without the CD, keeping the actions going.

BLUE

TUNE
A   B A G
Stamp your feet and

Stamp and clap – Clap and stamp

- Listen to this version of *Stamp and clap* (*track 44*):

Stamp your feet and clap your hands,
Stamp your feet and clap your hands,
Stamp your feet and clap your hands,
We'll stamp and clap.

Clap your hands and stamp you feet,
Clap your hands and stamp you feet,
Clap your hands and stamp you feet,
We'll stamp and clap.

- Talk with the children about the reversed order of actions in the second verse. Perform both verses with the actions.

- Discuss other pairs of actions for this song, eg *Tap your knees and wiggle your fingers ...*

- Sing the song with one of the new pairs of actions and reverse the pattern in the second verse.

Stamp and clap

GREEN

RESOURCES
A variety of instruments and soundmakers to tap, scrape or shake.

TIP
Try contrasting vocal sounds, eg

First we shout and then we whisper...

Tap and scrape

- Sit in a circle with a selection of instruments and soundmakers in the middle.

- Sing *Stamp and clap* (*track 44*) to check that the children are familiar with it.

- Ask two children each to choose an instrument. In turn each child shows how their instrument may be played, eg

  – Selvia picks a tambour and taps it;

  – Ahad picks a guiro and scrapes it.

- Make up a new verse for *Stamp and clap* using the children's playing ideas, eg

First we tap and then we scrape...

- Sing the new song words as the pair of players make the sound to match the words. Everyone else mimes the playing action. Perform with or without the CD (*backing track 45*).

- Reverse the order of the sounds and perform a second verse:

First we scrape and then we tap...

GREY

TIP
Ask the children to contribute their own vocal sounds. Perhaps some could lead this echoing activity.

Sound parade

- Listen to *Sound parade* (*track 46*) and join in with the echoed vocal sounds:

Sound parade, sound parade,
Copy my sounds in the sound parade.

leader: Wheeeeee	*children:* Wheeeee
Mmmmmm	Mmmmmm
Sssssss	Sssssss
T-t-t-t	T-t-t-t

Sound parade, sound parade,
Did you copy my sounds in the sound parade?

- Listen to the second version of *Sound parade* (*track 47*) and echo the new changed order of sounds.

- Say the chant without the CD. Make up new vocal sounds for the children to copy, eg tongue clicks, cheek pops, lip pops, hums, *shshshshs, zzzzzzz,* etc.

- Repeat the new chant but change the order of echoed sounds.

- Extend the chant to include five or more vocal sounds.

Moving patterns

Musical focus: Structure   **Area of learning:** Mathematical development

YELLOW

RESOURCES
A tin of baked beans, box of eggs, bag of peas.

TUNE
E E E E
Go - ing to buy

TIP
Use real shopping items and a supermarket basket to make the song more realistic.

Help children to anticipate the next item in the song by pointing to it slightly ahead of singing it.

Supermarket song

- Sit in a circle with the three items from the song in the centre – a tin of baked beans, a box of eggs, and a bag of peas.

- Talk with the children about supermarket shopping, including any memories of sitting in the trolley and being pushed around.

- Listen to *Supermarket song* (*track 48, tune: One man went to mow*) and encourage the children to point to the items as they arise in the song.

Going to buy some food
At the supermarket,
One tin of baked beans,
Put it in the basket.

Going to buy some food
At the supermarket,
One tin of baked beans and a box of eggs,
Put them in the basket.

Going to buy some food
At the supermarket,
One tin of baked beans and a box of eggs and a bag of peas,
Put them in the basket.

BLUE

RESOURCES
Food shakers: transparent containers of pasta, pulses, rice, currants, etc.

TIP
Go supermarket shopping for the shaker materials with the children – and even sing *Supermarket song* there!

Supermarket shake-up

- Everyone sits in a circle with a food shaker. One child sits in the centre with the three shopping items named in *Supermarket song* and a basket.

- Everyone joins in singing *Supermarket song* (*track 48*) and the child in the centre puts the items in the basket as the song unfolds.

- All play the food shakers during the last line of the song to the rhythm of the words:

Put   them   in   the bas - ket.

Supermarket

GREEN

TIP
If a CD player is not available for use outside, play some squeaky trolley sounds on an instrument or other soundmaker, eg rub Indian bells together.

Trolley travels

- Sing *Supermarket song* together (*track 48*).

- Talk with the children about supermarkets – the long aisles and the need for trolleys.

- Everyone sits in a space. Explain that in this activity the children will be pushing an imaginary trolley round a supermarket, walking up and down in straight lines while the music of *Trolley travels* (*track 49*) plays. When the music stops (*press the pause button at any point in the music*), the children reach for an imaginary item and place it in their trolley. They may only start pushing their trolleys again when the music begins.

- At the end of the activity the children tell everyone which items they chose.

GREY

TUNE
E   E   E   E
Go-ing   to   buy

Music market

- Listen to *Music market* (*track 50, tune: One man went to mow*) and join in with the actions and sounds:

Going to buy some sounds
At the music market,
   One enormous stamp!
At the music market.

Going to buy some sounds
At the music market,
   One enormous stamp, patting knees,
At the music market.

Going to buy some sounds...
   One enormous stamp, patting knees, clapping hands,
At the music market.

Going to buy some sounds...
   One enormous stamp, patting knees, clapping hands,
   rubbing palms...

Going to buy some sounds...
   One enormous stamp, patting knees, clapping hands,
   rubbing palms, tapping toes,
At the music market.

- Practise the song several times to establish the cumulative pattern.

- Invent new sounds and actions from the children's suggestions.

Moving patterns

Musical focus: Structure   **Area of learning:** Mathematical development

YELLOW

RESOURCES
Five copies of the bicycle picture printed from the CD-ROM, cut out and pasted onto individual cards.

TUNE
D DC BD G
One wonky bicycle

TIP
Give each child a cardboard tube from a roll of clingfilm or foil to hold like handlebars, so that they can pretend to steer their 'wonky' machines.

BLUE

RESOURCES
Five chairs.

EXTENSION
Start with one rider but ask him or her to choose more than one companion. How many riders are there? Count, then sing the song with the appropriate number.

Five wonky bicycles

- Show the children the picture of the 'wonky bike', pointing out the bent wheels and the flat tyres.

- Listen to *Five wonky bicycles* (*track 51, tune: John Brown's body*) and invite the children to sit and jiggle about like wobbly riders.

- Ask a child to hold up one picture and encourage the others to join in with the first verse by singing and jiggling about on their 'wonky bikes'.

One wonky bicycle went riding round the town,
One wonky bicycle went riding round the town,
One wonky bicycle went riding round the town,
Then along came another bike to cycle round.

- The picture-holder chooses a friend to hold up a second picture as everyone sings:

Two wonky bicycles went riding round the town...
...Then along came another bike to cycle round.

- Continue adding verses up to five with matching numbers of pictures. The fifth verse ends with:

Five wonky bicycles went riding round the town...
...There were five wonky bicycles to cycle round.

Five wonky bicycle seats

- Sit in a circle with five chairs lined up one behind the other in the centre.

- Choose one child to sit back to front on the last chair in the row with hands holding the back of the chair like handlebars.

- Sing the first verse of *Five wonky bicycles* with or without the CD. Encourage everyone to mime holding their bike's handlebars and jiggle from side to side on their wonky bikes as they sing.

- At the end of verse one, pause and ask the first child to choose a friend to ride behind him on the next chair.

- Repeat the song until there are five riders in the centre. Ask the children to count the riders out loud.

Bicycle counting

Five squeaky bicycles

- Sit in a circle with a selection of instruments and soundmakers in the centre. Revise the song *Five wonky bicycles* (*track 51*).

- Ask one child to choose a sound for a squeaky bike. While the others sing a new version of *Five wonky bicycles*, the child plays the chosen squeaky bike sound. Encourage the player to respond freely to the music, eg the child might play a steady beat, the rhythm of the words or play on individual words or phrases at will:

One squeaky bicycle went riding round the town...

- Ask another child to choose another sound for a second squeaky bike and join in with the first child, playing the two different sounds freely while the others sing.

Two squeaky bicycles went riding round the town...

- Continue adding players and sounds, always corresponding to the number of bicycles. Help the children match instruments one-to-one to the number of bicycle riders.

Count back bikes

- All listen to *Count back bikes* (*track 52, tune: John Brown's body*), a new version of *Five wonky bicycles*, in which the bicycles are counted back from five to one. Join in singing when it is familiar:

Five wonky bicycles went riding round the town,
Five wonky bicycles went riding round the town,
Five wonky bicycles went riding round the town,
But one fell apart and landed on the ground!

Four wonky bicycles went riding round the town...

last verse:
One wonkey bicycle went riding round the town...
But that fell apart and landed on the ground!

- Stand in a circle and select five pairs of children. As everyone else sings *Count back bikes,* one child in each pair rides round the centre while the partner plays a chosen soundmaker.

- At the end of each verse, call out the name of a rider, who tumbles to the ground then sits quietly in the centre with his or her partner.

- Repeat until all the bicycles have fallen apart.

Working world

Musical focus: *Texture* **Area of learning:** *Knowledge and understanding of the world*

RESOURCES
A colourful litter bin.

TUNE
D D D F♯
Don't drop lit-ter

TIP
Repeat with alternative actions such as tapping shoulders to the beat instead of marching.

Don't drop litter

- The children stand in a circle round a colourful litter bin. Listen to *Don't drop litter* (*track 1, tune: Ten green bottles*), encouraging the children to march on the spot to the beat of the song:

Don't drop lit-ter – put it in the bin...

- When they can march securely to the beat, add another action – on the word bin stop marching and point to the bin.

- When the song is familiar, encourage the children to join you in singing it with or without the CD, adding the actions:

Don't drop litter – put it in the bin,
Don't drop litter – put it in the bin,
Let's keep our playground tidy, neat and clean,
So don't drop litter – put it in the bin.

BLUE

RESOURCES
A collection of clean packaging materials and wrappers, eg crisp packets, cardboard cartons and tubes.

TUNE
D D D F♯
No crisp packets

TIP
Encourage children and parents to explore sounds together using packaging materials at home. These may be brought in and new verses created with them.

Crisp packet players

- Explore together the many different sounds you can make using a variety of packaging materials and playing actions like crumpling, tapping, flicking, twisting, rubbing, shaking, tearing, stroking, etc.

- When the children are familiar with *Don't drop litter* (*track 1*), listen to and join in with marching and pointing actions in this new verse (*track 2*):

No crisp packets – put them in the bin,
No crisp packets – put them in the bin,
Let's keep our playground tidy, neat and clean,
So no crisp packets – put them in the bin.

- Sing the new verse again and invite individual children to make sounds they have explored with crisp packets on the words 'put them in the bin'.

- Make up new verses for the different packaging items, adding the sounds they can make on the words 'put them in the bin', eg:

No biscuit wrappers – put them in the bin...

Sing the new verses with or without the CD (*backing track 3*).

Litter

GREEN

EXTENSIONS

Occasionally, ask a child to pull out two wrappers and make two sounds. Two other children match these sounds with instruments and create texture by playing them together.

Hide a set of instruments behind a screen. Invite a child to play one of the instruments with a twisting, flicking, tapping, or rubbing action. The others show with their hands how the sound was made.

Litter bag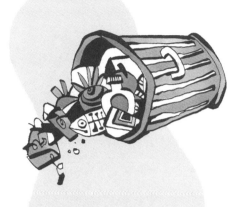

- Revise with the children the variety of sounds they can make from paper or cellophane wrapping (*explored in* BLUE *level*). Seat the children in a circle with a selection of percussion instruments placed in the centre.

- Pass a bag filled with empty, clean and dry wrappers round the circle while you all say this chant:

Here's a bag to feel inside,
Piece of litter, you can't hide.

- When the chant ends, the child holding the bag pulls out a wrapper and makes a sound with it, using an action such as twisting, rubbing, flicking, or tapping. The child sitting next in the circle selects an instrument from the centre and plays a sound, using a similar action, eg

    - twisting a maraca;

    - rubbing a tambour head;

    - flicking a set of jingles;

    - tapping a woodblock.

- Repeat the activity until a variety of instruments and playing methods have been explored and everyone has had a turn.

GREY

RESOURCES

A colourful litter bin.

A collection of clean, dry litter, eg cardboard tubes, plastic bottles, wrappers, empty biscuit tins, chocolate trays, cellophane, paper, etc.

Litter muncher

- Talk with the children about litter bins and the weekly bin collection at school and at home. Some children may be able to talk about recycling materials.

- Say this chant together, using hands and arms as jaws to open and close in big actions on the beat:

The big   litter   muncher comes rumbling down the street,
Its jaws are o - pen   ve - ry wide   finding things to   eat.

- The children stand in a line with a colourful bin full of litter soundmakers at one end. Invite the children one after the other, to choose a soundmaker and make a sound. Encourage them to try a variety of fast, slow, loud and quiet sounds.

- When each child has a litter soundmaker, all begin making sounds to the beat of the chant as you say the words. Practice playing very quietly at the beginning of the chant and getting louder till all stop on 'eat'.

- Choose a child to be the 'litter muncher', which moves along the line, pretending to scoop up the litter. As the litter muncher passes by, each sound stops as it is gobbled up. Repeat the chant until all the sounds are gone.

Working world

Musical focus: *Texture*   Area of learning: *Knowledge and understanding of the world*

YELLOW

RESOURCES
If possible show the children a transparent toy machine with a visible mechanism.

TUNE
C F F F A C
Today I made a fine

TIP
Some children may be able to move and sing the song at the same time.

My machine – first verse

- Show the children a toy machine such as a train with moving parts. Listen to **My machine** (*track 4, tune: The wheels on the bus*), joining in with the singing when ready:

Today I made a fine machine,
Fine machine, fine machine.
Today I made a fine machine,
See it work.

- Model the beat for the children, using a machine-like action, eg tap fist on fist like a mechanical hammer.

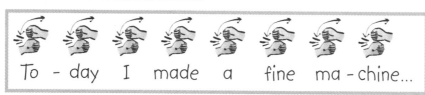

- Observe the movements of the toy machine and ask the children to demonstrate some of them with their bodies, eg moving a hand up and down like a piston, raising and lowering an arm like a lever, moving upper bodies from side to side like a digger.

- As you play the CD again, encourage the children to choose a movement and perform it to the beat of the song.

BLUE

TUNE
C F F F A C
Today I made a fine

My machine – complete

- Everyone sits in a space. Listen to **My machine** (*track 5*) several times and join in with the actions for each verse. Encourage them to join in the singing when ready.

Today I made a fine machine...

The wheels go round on my machine,
My machine, my machine,
The wheels go round on my machine
See them turn.

The door slams shut on my machine...
See it slam.

The springs can stretch on my machine...
See them stretch.

Now my machine is very tired...
It slows right down.

- When the song and actions are familiar, encourage the children to move around the space, performing one of the machine actions as they sing the verses. During the last verse the children slow their movements down gradually to a standstill.

GREEN

RESOURCES
A collection of wind-up, battery-operated and mechanical toys.

A variety of instruments, eg maraca, Indian bells, cylindrical shaker (chocolo), tambourine.

EXTENSION
Set three toys working and ask three children to match their movements with sounds.

Moving toys

- Sing *My machine* together. Each child chooses one action to perform throughout the song, starting it when their verse starts and continuing through to the end, when all slow down and stop.

- Show the children a collection of moving toys, putting them into operation one by one.

- Talk with the children about how each toy moves – some may rotate, tap an object, turn over, stop and start, and so on.

- Ask each child to choose an instrument that can be played with a similar movement to one of the toys, eg

  – rotate: maraca;

  – tap: Indian bells;

  – tip from side to side: cylindrical shaker;

  – shake then hold still: tambourine.

- Ask each child in turn to play their chosen instrument as the corresponding toy operates.

- Choose two toys and two children to play their matching sounds. Start each toy moving in turn. As their toys begin to move, the children start making their toy's sound, continuing until the toys are stopped, either together or one at a time.

- Record the activity, asking all the children to listen to and talk about what they hear (*sometimes the sounds are heard on their own, sometimes together*).

GREY

RESOURCES
A duster.

A print out of the story from the CD-ROM.

TUNE
A B A G
Time to clean and

TIP
Record the storytelling and play it back, noticing how the sounds of the toys become more complex as more are set in motion.

The little toymaker

- Listen to *The little toymaker* (*track 6*).

- Talk about the toys in the story. What kind of actions might they make? With the children explore and practise short, whole body movement sequences typical of a mechanical or articulated toy, eg

  – spinning top: hands on head press down three times, then spin quickly round on the spot;

  – digger: hold hands and arms out like a scoop, raise arms in short, sharp jerks, then tip in smooth arc over shoulders;

  – puppet: step forward on 'strings' for four steps, tip whole body forward and waggle arms loosely.

- From a range of instruments and soundmakers find ways of playing, which mirror the movement patterns you have explored, eg

  – spinning top: scraper – three very short, sharp scrapes, followed by fast circular rubbing;

  – digger: maraca – raise maraca in quick jerks, then shake loosely back down;

  – puppet: tambourine – tap rim gently four times, brush the skin with the palm, then shake loosely.

- Retell the story together. You are the toymaker who dusts the toys and sets them working one at a time. While some children play the sound sequences of the toys, beginning when you 'dust' them, the others sing the toymaker's song, *Time to clean and dust my toys* (*Polly put the kettle on*), with you.

Working world

Musical focus: Texture   **Area of learning:** Knowledge and understanding of the world

YELLOW

TUNE
D   E   F♯ G

When we're on the

TIP
Use a different action to represent a farm activity such as digging, sowing, or raking each time the verse is sung.

When we're on the farm – first verse

- All listen to, then join in singing the first verse of *When we're on the farm* (track 7):

When we're on the farm,
When we're on the farm,
Follow us, we'll lead the way,
Show the animals where they stay,
When we're on the farm.

- When the children become familiar with the song, encourage them to join you in marking the beat by tapping or clapping:

When we're on   the farm ...

BLUE

RESOURCES
A selection of instruments and soundmakers, eg ocean drum or tube shaker, tambourine, maraca, etc.

TUNE
D   E   F♯ G
Pig has lost his

When we're on the farm – complete

- In a large space, encourage the children to join in singing all the verses of the song (track 8), adding a different animal movement to each instrumental repeat of the verse:

Pig has lost his sty
Pig has lost his sty
Follow us, we'll lead the way
Show the pig where he can stay
When we're on the farm.   *(slowly searching, head swaying side to side)*

Chicken has lost her coop...   *(stopping and starting, arms flapping as wings)*

Horse has lost his stable...   *(holding bridle, hands moving up and down)*

Sheep has lost his pen...   *(gentle circling)*

Rabbit has lost his hutch...   *(hopping and stopping)*

Cow has lost her byre...   *(gentle, slow plod)*

Duck has lost her pond...   *(head held high, waddling hands)*

- Help the children find ways of using a variety of instruments to mirror the animal movements, eg

  – pig: an ocean drum or tube shaker, gently swayed from side to side;
  – hen: quick shakes of a tambourine to one side then to the other;
  – horse: stick maraca tapped into the palm.

- Sing and move to the song with or without the CD, while a few children play the chosen sounds during the instrumental verses.

Farm time

GREEN

RESOURCES
Instruments as
in BLUE level.

Enlarged print
out of the two
farm layouts on
the CD-ROM
(attach these
side by side to
make one).

Print out, cut up
and paste onto
cards the six
animal pictures
on the CD-ROM.

Farm homes

- Revise the song *When we're on the farm* without the CD, adding the actions and accompanying the singing with instruments.

- Sit in a circle with groups of animal players next to each other: chickens, pigs, ducks, etc. Place an enlarged picture of the farm layout in the centre of the circle.

- Pass a box or tray containing the animal cards round the circle as you all sing the first verse of *When we're on the farm*. The child holding the box at the end of the verse is the farmer.

- The farmer picks one of the cards and holds it for the others to see. All sing the appropriate verse of *When we're on the farm*, while the animal group plays and the farmer places the animal card in its home on the farm layout.

- Pass the box round as you sing again to choose a new farmer.

GREY

RESOURCES
Six groups of
instruments, eg
woodblocks,
maracas, chime
bars, guiros,
cymbals, hand
drums.

Coloured hoops.

Masks and farm
tools made by
the children.

TIP
Encourage the
farmer's group to
change direction
in their route.

Place the CD-
ROM pictures of
the farm layout
and animal cards
with a selection
of instruments in
the music corner
where individuals
can continue
with this
mapping activity.
Encourage the
children to find
their own sounds
for each animal
in its home.

Farm procession

- In a large space, place different groups of instruments in coloured hoops (*eg woodblocks in one, guiros in another*).

- With the children, try out the sounds of the instruments and decide which would suit each of the six animals. Place the animal cards in the hoops to identify them. Invite the children to select an 'animal home' and sit next to it.

- A small group of farm workers, led by the farmer, make a procession around the farm. As they pause at each of the animal's homes, the children greet the group with their musical sounds and stop playing as the procession moves on.

- Vary the texture of the music by asking the farmer's group to split up and make their way by different routes.

Working world

Musical focus: *Texture* Area of learning: *Knowledge and understanding of the world*

YELLOW

RESOURCES
A toy robot, doll or puppet with jointed limbs.

TUNE
B E F♯ G♯
I'm walk-ing like

TIP
Make a collection of robotic toys, including some from home to create a robot museum for the children to explore.

I'm walking like a robot

- Everyone listens to *I'm walking like a robot* (*track 9, tune: Poor Jenny sits a weeping*). During the each verse, move the parts of a toy robot to match the actions in the song, inviting the children to join in:

I'm walking like a robot, a robot, a robot,
I'm walking like a robot, just look at me now,

My head turns in a circle, in a circle, in a circle,
My head turns in a circle, just look at me now.

My eyes are big and wobbly...

My arms move very stiffly...

My ears are very wiggley...

My hands are very jerky...

My legs are very bendy...

My feet are slow and heavy...

I'm walking like a robot...

- Sing or play the song again, encouraging the children to join in with the repeated words as they become familiar.

BLUE

RESOURCES
A toy robot.

EXTENSION
Make up new verses for other parts of the robot's body, eg wires, fingers, teeth, ankles, voice, etc.

I'm moving like a robot

- Talk with the children about a robot toy's actions and the quality of the movements – stiff, slow, jerky, heavy, and so on.

- Explore and create sequences of movements with the children to show the robot's activities, such as swivelling the head in a series of slow, smooth movements, raising arms stiffly as if moving a large object, slow and deliberate footsteps in a sideways direction as if moving round an object, and so on.

- Explore corresponding sequences of vocal sounds to match the robot's movement sequences, eg

  – swivelling head: zhhhhhh–tk, zhhhhhh–tk, zhhhhhh–tk;

  – raising arms: sssssss ssssssss   sssssssssss sssssssss;

  – footsteps: crunk   crunk   crunk   crunk.

- Ask the children to join in singing *I'm walking like a robot* with or without the CD (*track 9*). Invite individuals or pairs of children to perform the appropriate vocal sound sequence after each verse.

- Encourage individuals to make up a longer sequence of robotic movements, linking two or more vocal sound sequences.

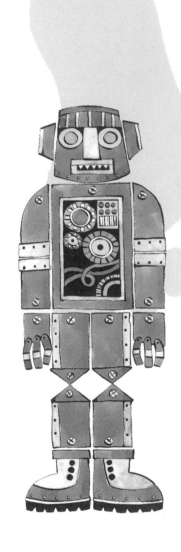

Robot

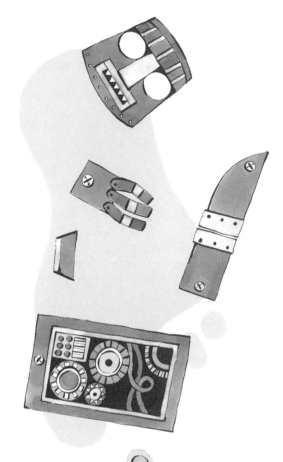

Robot builders

- Sing *I'm walking like a robot* (*track 9*) and revise moving in stiff, jerky and spikey ways.

- Show the children the robot body cards and identify together which cards show the legs, arms, hands, body, head, ears and eyes.

- The children sit in a circle with a collection of metallic instruments and sound sources in the middle. Help the children to explore sounds for each part of the robot's body, eg

    – quick taps on tambourine for wobbly eyes; scratching guiro sounds for bending arms; clinking washer sounds for wiggley ears; hard, strong scraping sounds for stiff walking legs.

- Place all the cards face down in the centre of the circle. Invite one child to turn over a card, and find a robotic movement to perform for that part of the body. Invite another child to select a soundmaker to accompany the movement.

- Invite another child to turn up another card and place it in correct relation to the first. While this child performs an appropriate robotic movement for that part of the body, another child selects and plays an accompanying sound.

- Continue until all the parts of the robot's body have been performed in turn and placed correctly in relation to each other.

- Play all the metallic body sounds together when the robot is complete.

Mending the Iron Man

- Listen to *The Iron Man* (*track 10*).

- In the story, the Iron Man breaks into separate pieces. Explain that the children need to make a piece of music to put the Iron Man's body back together again.

- Remind the children of the sounds and movements they found for the different parts of a robot's body (BLUE and GREEN levels). Divide into small groups, seated next to each other in a large circle. Allocate a part of the body to each group.

- In their groups, the children practise making the sound for their part of the Iron Man's body.

- Place the set of robot cards face down in the centre of the ring. Select one child to be the robot builder. When this child turns over a robot card, the corresponding group begins to play and continues playing while the next card is turned over and the next group begins. The robot builder puts the cards in relation to each other and may make the piece of accompanying music as long or as short as they like according to how quickly they build the robot.

- To finish your piece of rebuilding music, direct the groups to make their sounds get quieter and quieter, as the rebuilt Iron Man walks away along the beach into the distance.

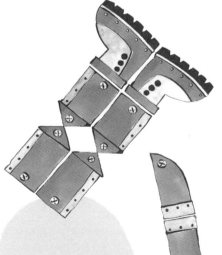

GREEN

RESOURCES
Print out the colour pictures of the robot on the CD-ROM. Cut out the separate parts of the body and paste them onto card.

Collect metallic sound sources, eg pairs of cymbals, cooling tray and fork, washers, multi-guiro, tambourine, milk bottle tops.

TIP
Form groups of three or four and ask the children to combine several sounds for each body movement.

GREY

RESOURCES
A set of robot body cards.

A selection of metallic instruments and sound sources.

A print out of the story from the CD-ROM.

TIP
Make a large, articulated robot from the CD-ROM pictures for display in the setting.

Record a performance of the story followed by the rebuilding music on video or cassette and talk about what the children liked and felt was effective.

Working world

Musical focus: Texture   Area of learning: Knowledge and understanding of the world

YELLOW

RESOURCES
A gardening book or magazine, illustrated in colour.

TUNE
D D E F#
Hel-lo, Mis-ter

TIP
Make a colourful collage of a garden with tissue paper flowers and vegetables laid out in the colour order of the rainbow.

Hello, Mr Sun

- Standing in their own space, the children listen to *Hello, Mr Sun* (*track 11*), following the practitioner performing the actions:

Hello, Mr Sun, hello, hello.   (wave arms side to side above head in time to the music)
Hello, Mister Sun, hello.
Shine down, shine down,   (raise arms above head and sweep them out to sides in smooth arc)
And make my flowers grow.   (raise hands palms up from low to high)

Hello, Mister Sun, hello, hello.
Hello, Mister Sun, hello.
Shine down, shine down,
And make my tulips grow.

Hello, Mister Sun, hello, hello...
And make my buttercups grow.

- Listen to the song again, encouraging the children to join in the singing when they are ready.

- Ask the children the names of flowers and plants they know. Show them a gardening book for extra ideas, noticing the colours of the flowers and vegetables. Can they find one to match each colour of the rainbow? Make up new verses for the song with the suggestions from the children.

- Talk about the importance of the sun for growing things.

- Sing the song with the actions out of doors on a sunny day.

BLUE

RESOURCES
Bright-sounding, non-sustaining instruments such as woodblocks, tambourines, cabasa.

Gentle-sounding, sustaining instruments such as glockenspiel, tone bar, Indian cymbals.

TUNE
C G G A
Oh Moon, would you

Ghoom–parani gaan

- Talk with the children about the difference between the light of day when the sun shines and the darkness of night when the moon comes out.

- Listen to the lullaby, *Oh, moon – Ghoom-parani gaan* (*track 12*) and encourage the children to join in with the singing.

Oh Moon, would you come and play with me today? x2
Would you bring your golden boat and take me far away? x2

Aey chand, amaar sathe khelbi jodi aey, x2
Amay nie jaarea ji tor shonar naye. x2

- Help the children to explore voices, instruments and sound sources which can make lively, bright, fast-moving sounds to represent activities during the day, such as quick, sharp tapping on woodblocks, lively irregular beats on tambourine and cabasa.

- Contrast the bright daytime sounds with quiet, peaceful, calm sounds that represent the still night when they sleep, eg long, slow strokes on a glockenspiel, a sustained note on a tone bar, single taps on Indian cymbals..

GREEN

RESOURCES
A display of rainbow-coloured items including some from home.

A print out of the poem from the CD-ROM.

TIP
With the children paint a large rainbow as a backdrop to the display of rainbow-coloured items

Rainbow dreams is a guided meditation which may be used at rest time to help create a calm and sleepy atmosphere.

Rainbow dreams

- With the children, group different coloured items into a rainbow display. Talk about each group in turn and the colour it represents.

- Read or play the recording of *Rainbow dreams* (*track 13*). Together, match the coloured items appropriately to each verse.

- Explore slow, peaceful actions to illustrate the verses, eg

  – orange: big, circular sun, body shapes with arms which gradually becoming lower and lower;

  – green: stroke the fur of the rabbit.

GREY

RESOURCES
A camcorder.

A large painted rainbow as suggested in GREEN level.

A range of soundmakers.

CD-ROM videoclip and whiteboard.

TIP
Some children may be able to listen again to *Rainbow dreams* on track 65 and compare the ways the background music on the recording is the same or different from their own.

Rainbow sounds

- Listen to *Rainbow dreams* (*track 13*) and talk about the colours and events in each verse.

- Using voices and a variety of instruments and sound sources, help the children to explore sounds to illustrate each verse, eg

  – yellow: gentle wing flapping with large piece of paper; moonlight sounds played gently on metallic instruments such as glockenspiel and triangle.

- Read the verses of the poem in turn and ask some children to perform actions and other children to play instruments as an accompaniment.

- Film the children making their music, then ask them to watch and listen to it, and suggest ways in which they could use their instruments and bodies more expressively to create the calm mood of night and a sleepy atmosphere, eg each sound might be played more slowly, more quietly, and for a longer time.

- Use a painted rainbow to conduct a performance of the music. As you point to the red band of colour, the children make their actions and sounds for red. As you slowly move your fingertip towards orange, the sounds and actions change to this colour, and so on.

- Alternatively, show the children the CD-ROM rainbow videoclip (*C3*) projected onto a screen or whiteboard if available. This display of gradually changing coloured light may be accompanied by the music you have created for each colour.

Working world

Musical focus: Texture   **Area of learning:** Knowledge and understanding of the world

The world's at work

- Sit in a circle. As you say the chant, *The world's at work*, pass round the circle a cloth bag containing models and toys of working people:

> While we sleep
> And while we play
> The world's at work
> Through night and day.

- At the end of the rhyme, one child chooses an item from the bag and places it for everyone to see. With your guidance, the children name the toy and talk about the work of the helper it represents.

- Repeat the activity until all the items are on display.

Sounds helpful

- The children chant *The world's at work*, choosing and displaying an item from the prepared toy bag after each repeat.

- Encourage the children to share their understanding of the people represented by the toys, such as the policewoman walking the beat, or fire-fighter climbing a ladder, and so on.

- Help the children to find actions and to create vocal sounds, body percussion or instrumental sounds to represent these activities, eg

  - street sweeping: vocal 'swish'; brush hand across clothing; rub sandpaper blocks together;

  - climbing a ladder: rising tongue clicks; raise one arm straight above head and tap it with the other from shoulder up to fingertips; tap the notes of a xylophone from low to high;

  - ambulance: vocal 'neenaw', and so on.

- All the children say the chant together. At the end, invite a child to select an item from the bag. Invite another child to choose and make a representative sound from those explored. Repeat until all the items have been displayed and represented in sound.

GREEN

RESOURCES
A print out of the story from the CD-ROM.

TUNE

B   E F♯ G A
I'm look-ing for a

TIP
If you have an electronic keyboard with pre-set sounds, help children to explore those which link with the emergency services.

Foxy comes to town (14-15)

- Talk with the children about the sounds of the city at night, in particular mentioning the emergency services and other public service workers.

- Listen to *Foxy comes to town* (*track 14, text on CD-ROM*).

- All sing foxy's song together (*track 15*):

I'm looking for a dustbin, a dustbin, a dustbin,
I'm looking for a dustbin in the middle of town.

- All together, explore vocal sounds to match the sounds of the street sweeper, the ambulance, fire engine, police woman's feet, and the crashing dustbins.

- You tell foxy's story. Everyone sings foxy's song and joins in with the vocal night time sounds.

GREY

RESOURCES
Collection of instruments and soundmakers to accompany the story.

Foxy comes to town again (14)

- Listen to *Foxy comes to town* (*track 14*).

- Using a variety of instruments and soundmakers, help the children to explore and create sounds they could use to accompany *Foxy's song*, eg

  – real dustbin lid tapped with a wooden spoon;

  – tapped tambourine or cymbal.

Play these sounds on the beat or more freely, eg (*beat*)

I'm look - ing for a dust - bin,   a...

- Explore vocal sounds, body percussion, instruments and soundmakers for the night time sounds of the street sweeper, the ambulance, fire engine, police woman's feet, and the crashing dustbins.

- Make a grand performance for parents, carers and other children. Retell the story with added sounds and sing the song with its accompaniment.

Musical focus: Loud and quiet   **Area of learning:** Physical development

There's a quiet caterpillar on a leaf

- Read *The hungry caterpillar* by Eric Carle to the children, showing them the illustrations.

- Listen to *There's a tiny caterpillar* (track 16, tune: *She'll be coming round the mountain*), encouraging the children to join in with the hand actions and the whispered words.

Vs1 Tiny caterpillar
 – wiggle wiggle

Vs2 Eat the leaves
 – munch munch

Vs3 Spinning a cocoon
 – spin spin

Vs4 Butterfly
 – flap, flap

Caterpillar caper

- Ask the children to:

  – Verse 1: lie down and use their whole bodies to wriggle like a caterpillar;

  – Verse 2: hold a partner's hands and together make a huge mouth that opens and closes;

  – Verse 3: stand on the spot and make turning, spinning movements;

  – Verse 4: move about freely lifting arms up and down like delicate wings.

- Perform the dance using the song, *There's a tiny caterpillar*, as an accompaniment. Either sing the song yourself or use the CD. Stop between verses if necessary, to remind the children about the next movement.

Caterpillar

There's a tiny caterpillar on a leaf

• Encourage the children to sing *There's a tiny caterpillar* with you without the CD.

Vs1 There's a tiny caterpillar on a leaf – wiggle, wiggle,
There's a tiny caterpillar on a leaf – wiggle, wiggle,
There's a tiny caterpillar, tiny caterpillar,
There's a tiny caterpillar on a leaf – wiggle, wiggle.

Vs2 He will eat the leaves around him 'til he's full –
munch, munch...

Vs3 A cocoon is what he's spinning for his home –
spin, spin...

Vs4 Then he'll be a butterfly and fly away – flap, flap...

• Sit in a circle with a selection of instruments and soundmakers.

• Ask four children in turn to make up a quiet sound on an instrument to match the action words– 'wiggle,' 'munch' 'spin' and 'flap'.

• Perform the song without the CD using instrument sounds and hand actions.

Caterpillar caterpillar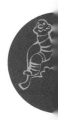

• Listen to *There's a tiny caterpillar* (track 16)

• Listen to *Caterpillar caterpillar* (track 17) noticing together how each line gets louder and louder:

Caterpillar caterpillar, wriggle about,
Caterpillar caterpillar, growing stout,
Caterpillar caterpillar, spin your cocoon,
Caterpillar caterpillar, butterfly soon!

• Encourage the children to join in with the words 'caterpillar, caterpillar' matching their voices to the voice on the CD.

• Say the whole chant without the CD.

• Stand in a circle and tap knees on the repeated words 'caterpillar, caterpillar' each time they come. Match the quietness or loudness of the knee taps to the voices.

Ca - ter - pil - lar,   ca - ter - pil - lar...

• Think of actions to accompany the other words and perform the whole chant.

Growth and change

Musical focus: Loud and quiet   **Area of learning:** Physical development

YELLOW

RESOURCES
Access to a water tap.

Computer access to view or print out the interactive picture.

Tap talk

- Talk with the children about water taps in their kitchens and bathrooms. Show them the taps on the CD-ROM and give opportunities for them to play with the interactive picture.

- Gather the children round a real tap. Encourage them to listen carefully with eyes closed to the sound of the tap dripping then gushing.

- Listen to the recorded sounds of tap water (*track 18*) and talk about different water sounds from quiet dripping to loud gushing. Encourage the children to make quiet tongue clicks to imitate the gentle sounds made by the dripping tap on the CD, and change to a loud, vocal 'swish' for the gushing sounds of a flowing tap.

- Encourage the children to respond to what they hear with movement, eg

    – dripping: quiet tiptoe steps;

    – gushing: running round freely, letting their feet make louder sounds on the floor.

BLUE

TUNE
G E G
Our tap drips

TIP
Be careful not to confuse fast sounds with loud sounds, and slow with quiet. Fast may also be quiet, and slow may also be loud.

EXTENSION
Make up new verses for the song which use quiet, fast, rushing sounds, and loud, slow, dripping sounds.

Our tap drips

- Listen to *Our tap drips* (*track 19*, tune: *This old man*):

Our tap drips – drip, drip, drip,
Water's trickling – slip, slip, slip,
Running quietly,
Water on its way,
Listen to our tap today:
    Tck, tck, tck, tck, tck, tck, tck.

Our tap pours – gush, gush, gush,
Water's splashing – rush, rush, rush,
Running loudly,
Water on its way,
Listen to our tap today:
    Swish._____

- Remind the children of the variety of sounds made by tap water using CD track 18 or a real tap.

- Practise making light tongue clicks for quiet dripping sounds. Say 'swish' loudly for the sound of forceful, gushing water.

- Encourage the children to join in with the song, making the first verse very quiet and the second verse much louder. Add the vocal 'tck tck' and 'swish' sounds.

Tap talk

GREEN

RESOURCES
A tambour.

EXTENSION
Encourage the children to explore movement further by giving them the opportunity to respond freely to the sounds on CD track 3. Encourage the full use of a large indoor space, and a wide range of body movement.

GREY

RESOURCES
Instruments and soundmakers such as xylophone, bells, maracas, corrugated card, tissue paper, yoghurt pots.

TIP
Encourage children without instruments to make contrasting hand actions to match the quiet and loud sounds they hear - eg dancing fingers for quiet sounds and tapped fists for loud sounds.

EXTENSION
Investigate some other ways to play watery sounds for new verses.

Tap dance

- Listen to the song *Our tap drips* (*track 19*). Remind the class of the variety of sounds that tap water makes (*track 18*).

- With the children, explore ways of making a quiet, fast, dripping sound, using fingers or a soft beater on a tambour, eg

  – tap very quickly and lightly on the tambour skin.

  Invite the children to stand in their own space. When you play the chosen tambour sound, the children respond by tapping in the same way with their fingertips on different parts of their body like the drips from the tap.

- Now explore playing loud, fast, rushing water sounds on the tambour, eg

  – scrape your fingernails in a smooth, circular motion round the tambour skin.

  Invite the children to respond with large, swirling body movements.

- Alternate between the quiet and loud sounds on the tambour, encouraging the children to listen and respond with the appropriate movements.

Our tap drips – water music

- Sit in a circle with a selection of instruments and soundmakers in the centre.

- Explore instrumental sounds which can be found to make a variety of tap water sounds.

- Sing *Our tap drips* together. Invite a few children to make up quiet 'drip' sounds on some of the instruments to describe the quiet sounds in verse one, eg finger taps on drums, nails scratched across corrugated card, or tearing paper slowly.

- Invite another group to make up loud 'gushing' water sounds for verse two, eg beaters running up and down a xylophone, or bells and maracas shaken vigorously.

- Sing the song without the CD, directing the two groups to play their sounds at the end of the appropriate verse.

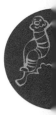

Growth and change

Musical focus: Loud and quiet   **Area of learning:** Physical development

YELLOW

RESOURCES
Winter items and references.

TIP
Make some ice and let the children examine it by touching and tasting it. Look at the crystals through a microscope and watch it melt.

The snow is dancing

- Ask parents to contribute postcards, posters, pictures or books that depict snowy scenes. Use these to make a winter table, adding a collection of warm clothing or winter sports equipment.

- Listen to **The snow is dancing** (*track 20*) and show the children the videoclip animation on the CD-ROM. As they listen to the music encourage the children to improvise a finger dance of snowflakes.

- Show the children the bear illustration on this page. Talk about the brown bear's long winter sleep while snow covers the land, and about his spring awakening.

- Listen to **Brown bear's snoring** (*track 21*). Encourage the children to join in with the snoring and with these actions:

  - bear sleeping: rest cheek on hands;

  - snow and ice are melting, icicles are dropping: dance fingertips from high to low;

  - ears are listening: cup hands round ears;

  - eyes begin to peep: make circles with first fingers and thumbs round eyes.

BLUE

RESOURCES
A variety of metallic instruments such as jingles and Indian cymbals.

TUNE
C C C E
Brown bear's snoring

TIP
The metallic instruments collection might include everyday sound makers from the kitchen, such as spoons to clink together, a saucepan and lid to rattle, an egg whisk or paperclips shaken on a metal plate.

Brown bear's snoring

- Sit in a circle with a selection of metallic instruments and soundmakers in the centre.

- Sing **Brown bear's snoring** with the CD (*track 21*), adding the hand actions and snores.

Brown bear's snoring, brown bear's snoring,
In his winter sleep – snore snore snore.
Brown bear's snoring, brown bear's snoring,
In his winter sleep – snore snore snore.
Snow and ice are melting,
Icicles are dropping,
Brown bear's ears are listening
And his eyes begin to peep.

- Ask a small group of children to choose instruments which can make quiet, 'icy' sounds and to play them during the instrumental repeat of the song, while the others sing or perform the actions.

GREEN

RESOURCES
Metallic
instruments and
a tambour.

TIP
Encourage the
children to join
in making loud
growling vocal
sounds and
using heavy,
loud feet as they
walk. A few
children may
join in playing
tambours for a
really loud
sound.

Send the bears
back to sleep by
gradually playing
the tambour
beat more
quietly and
resuming the icy
sounds.

Bear's waking up dance

- Listen to *Brown bear's snoring* (*track 21*) and perform the actions with the song, reminding the children of brown bear's winter sleep.

- Select three or four children to play instruments. All the others find a space and curl up like sleeping bears.

- The players choose metallic instruments on which to make very quiet snow and ice sounds. As the players move quietly among the 'sleeping bears' making their icy sounds, the children wake up, gently stretching limbs, making yawning faces and gradually sitting up to the quiet sounds.

- As you begin to play a quiet, steady beat on a tambour, the bears get up and walk all around on all fours. Gradually play louder beats on the tambour; the bears respond by becoming more lively and playful.

- If played indoors, CD track 22 may be used to accompany bear's waking up dance.

GREY

RESOURCES
Metallic
instruments and
a tambour.

TIP
Ask the children
to describe what
happens during
the chant (*the
chanting and
tambour get
louder and
louder*).

EXTENSION
Place a copy of
the brown bear
illustration in the
music corner
with metallic
instruments and
a tambour.
Encourage
individuals and
pairs of children
to tell brown
bear's story in
sound using the
instruments.

Brown bear chooses you!

- Sit in a circle with one child, the sleeping brown bear, curled up in the centre.

- Sing *Brown bear's snoring* without the CD, while a small group of children play 'icy' sounds on instruments.

- At the end of the song, the bear wakes up and walks on all fours around the inside of the ring. Everyone else chants while you play a steady tambour beat, beginning quietly and getting louder throughout:

Brown bear's choos - ing,

Brown bear's choos - ing,

Brown bear's choos - ing   YOU!

- On the word 'YOU', the bear points to the nearest child. She becomes the new 'bear' and the game starts again.

- Give the children turns to play the tambour.

Growth and change

Musical focus: Loud and quiet   **Area of learning:** Physical development

YELLOW

Storm

TIP
Talk to the
children about
their experiences
of stormy
weather and its
effects – what
damage can a
bad storm do?

When out of
doors, look at
clouds and talk
about what
happens to their
shapes and
colour when
there is a storm.

• Listen to the poem, *Storm* (*track 23*), and invite the children to join
in with the rain music by moving and wriggling their fingers like
dancing raindrops, first gently after verse one, then more vigorously
after verse two. After verse three bang palms on the floor to make
thunder music:

Summer's hot and summer's fun,
Everyone enjoys the sun,
But fluffy clouds are turning grey,
A storm is coming on its way.

(rain music – wriggle fingers)

Rain is falling from the sky,
Drumming on the passers by.
Thunder rumbles, can you hear?
A storm is getting very near!

(loud rain music – wriggle fingers and hands)

Puddles on the pavement grow,
Lightning flashes to and fro.
The sky grows black, the sun has fled,
A storm's arrived. It's overhead!

(thunder music – bang palms on floor)

BLUE

Conjure up a storm

TIP
The tapping
should be
random to
create an effect
of raindrops -
don't all clap a
steady beat.

Ask a child to be
the leader.

• Listen to *Storm* (*track 23*).

• Practise making quiet rain sounds, all tapping one finger on the
palm of the other hand. Now try tapping more loudly with three
fingers on the other palm to make heavier rain sounds.

• Lead the children in creating a piece of rain music using just fingers
and hands. Ask them to copy you:

   – tap one fingertip gently on the other palm;

   – gradually tap more loudly with more fingertips;

   – tap with the whole hand;

   – gradually go back to tapping with one fingertip.

• Try this again, checking that the children are listening and
responding to you.

• Record a performance. All listen back with eyes closed.

Storm

TIP
Encourage the
children to listen
to the sound of
their feet as
they move:
when the rain
gets louder,
their feet on the
ground get
louder too,
pounding and
drumming.
When the rain
grows quieter,
feet become
quieter.

Stormy sky dance

- Read the poem, *Storm*, encouraging the children to join in.

- Play *Stormy sky dance* (*track 24*), noticing the representation of rain, and thunder and lightning.

- Practise these whole body movements in a large space:
  – rain: move quickly around, weaving in and out of each other;
  – thunder and lightning: stand on the spot and make strong turning, twisting movements with hands clamped on opposite shoulders; contrast with sudden leaps, landing in jagged body shapes.

- Play *Stormy sky dance* again, adding the whole body movements. Encourage the children to respond as the thunder gets louder by making bigger and bigger body movements, turning and twisting, but still staying in one place.

Storm comes – storm goes

- Listen to *Storm* (*track 23*) and join in with it.

- Sit in a circle with a selection of instruments and soundmakers in the middle. Explore together some of the sounds they can make for gentle, harder and heavy rain, and for loud rumbles of thunder.

- Divide the class into two groups: rain and thunder. Allocate instruments to each group. If there are not enough for everyone, take turns with the instruments, using body percussion (*as explored in* BLUE *level*) as an alternative.

- Show the children the three weather cards: sun, rain and storm. Explain that when the sun card is shown, all are quiet. When they see the rain card, the rain group makes their sounds, and when the thunder card is displayed, the thunder group plays.

- Direct a performance using the weather cards:

  – all are quiet;

  – the rain group begin playing quietly then gradually more loudly (*move the card closer to the group to indicate getting louder*);

  – the storm group play loudly;

  – the rain group play moderately loudly then gradually get quieter (*move the card away from the group to indicate getting quieter*);

  – all are quiet.

- Discuss the effect of the music. Did everyone respond when their card was shown? How could the music be improved?

- Experiment with the weather cards, displaying rain and thunder together, or introducing a sudden sunny spell in the middle of the music.

RESOURCES
A variety of
instruments and
soundmakers,
eg shakers,
rattles, tubes,
drums, boxes.

Copies of the
three weather
cards: sun, rain
and storm,
printed out from
the CD-ROM
and pasted onto
card.

TIP
If you have a
parachute, divide
into two groups:
one, with
helpers, holds
the parachute
above the heads
of the seated
musicians. To
direct the
players, this
group starts to
waft the
parachute gently,
gradually making
it billow higher
and higher into
'storm clouds',
subsiding again
to direct the
music to
become quieter
then stop.

Musical focus: Loud and quiet   **Area of learning:** Physical development

YELLOW

RESOURCES
A print out of the CD-ROM pictures of cobwebs and ghosts.

TUNE
D C B D
In the hai - ry

TIP
Encourage the children to use their hands to make a megaphone shape around their mouths when they shout 'BOO'. Can they hear a difference?

The Hairy Scary Castle – tickle and shout

- Show the children the pictures on the CD-ROM of the cobwebs and ghosts that live in the *Hairy Scary Castle*.

- Listen to *The Hairy Scary Castle* (*track 25*) and encourage the children to join in with a loud 'BOO' at the end.

In the Hairy Scary Castle,
In the Hairy Scary Castle,
In the Hairy Scary Castle,
Where the cobwebs tickle
And the ghosts go BOO!

- Practise using fingertips to make quiet tickling sounds on faces, hands, arms, legs and the floor.

- Listen to the CD again, joining in with the tickling actions and sounds, and a loud 'BOO' at the end.

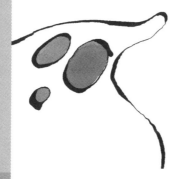

BLUE

RESOURCES
Make a collection of tube and funnel soundmakers such as tubes from foil or poster tubes.

Ask parents or your local supermarket to contribute clean, polystyrene food trays and plates.

If available, use a microphone, amplifier and speakers to demonstrate how the children's voices can sound when amplified electronically.

The Hairy Scary Castle – soundmakers

- Listen to *The Hairy Scary Castle* (*track 25*), joining in with the singing, adding tickling finger sounds and a loud 'BOO'.

- Talk with the children about how cobwebs are made and what they feel like. Let them share their ideas about ghosts.

- Encourage the children to shout 'BOO' through tubes and funnels, making their sounds really loud.

- Ask them to use their fingertips to make quiet, cobwebby, tickling sounds on polystyrene plates and food trays.

- Sing the song again, using the soundmakers to add tickling cobweb sounds and booing ghosts.

Boo!

Ghost dance

- Sing *The Hairy Scary Castle* (*track 25*).

- Talk about an imaginary room in the castle where the ghosts live. They sleep most of the time but if they hear footsteps, they jump out and shout 'Boo' then shrink back to sleep.

- Practise ghost jumps that grow from a small hunched-up shape and finish in a large, bold shape with arms stretched wide. Add a scary face with wide, staring eyes and don't forget to call 'BOO'! Shrink back to a small shape at the end.

- Now imagine walking through a room as quietly as possible, so that the ghosts don't wake up. Practise tiptoeing very quietly and carefully without making a sound!

- Divide the children into two groups. Listen to *Ghost dance* (*track 26*) and talk about which music belongs to the ghosts and which is the tiptoeing music.

- Play *Ghost dance* again. One group tiptoes and the other group becomes ghosts, ready in hunched-up shapes to jump out and call 'Boo'. Swap roles.

GREY

RESOURCES
A collection of instruments for making cobweb, ghost, and chain sounds.

TUNE
D C B D
In the hai - ry

TIP
Attach enlarged copies of the CD-ROM templates of cobwebs, ghosts, chains and monsters onto headbands for each group to wear to identify their characters.

The Hairy Scary Castle – chains and monsters too!

- Sit in a circle with a selection of instruments and soundmakers in the centre.

- Listen to the extended version of *The Hairy Scary Castle* (*track 27*):

In the Hairy Scary Castle...
Where the cobwebs tickle
And the ghosts go BOO!

In the Hairy Scary Castle...
Where the chains go clank,
And the monsters scream!
Where the cobwebs tickle
And the ghosts go BOO!

- Talk with the children about the sound that chains might make, dragging along the ground. Try out different soundmakers and ways of playing then choose the favourite.

- Ask the children for scary words for the monsters to scream. Practise making them really loud and terrifying.

- Revise the sounds explored in BLUE level for tickling cobwebs and ghosts.

- Divide into four groups: ghosts, cobwebs, chains and monsters and rehearse the song with the added sounds.

- Perform the song to an audience.

Growth and change

Musical focus: Loud and quiet   *Area of learning:* Physical development

YELLOW

RESOURCES
Access to a computer for the children to view the videoclip.

The king's birthday music

- Talk with the children about bands and the special occasions on which they play. Show them the videoclip of a marching band (*c5*).

- Listen to *The king's birthday music* (*track 28*) and talk about special things the children like doing at birthday parties.

- Play the story again, encouraging the children to join in with palms beating on knees when the drum plays loudly, and with quiet finger taps when it plays quietly.

BLUE

RESOURCES
Saucepans, plastic buckets, tubs and pots, tambours, tambourines, and a range of beaters, eg wooden and metal spoons, chop sticks, unsharpened pencils and short canes.

Large and small drum cards.

Loud and quiet drums

- Listen to the drumming at the end of *The king's birthday music* (*track 28*), tapping palms on knees, loudly and quietly in response to the drum as in YELLOW level.

- Sit in a circle with a selection of drum soundmakers and the large and small drum cards (*copied from the picture opposite*) and explore playing loudly and quietly on each soundmaker.

- Distribute a soundmaker to each child. Explain that when you show them the large drum card, they respond by playing loudly; when you show the small drum card they play quietly. When no card is shown they are silent.

Make sure that every child can see the signs clearly and give the children a lot of practice in responding to the loud and quiet signs.

The special drum

Wooden clogs and silk slippers

- Sit in a circle. Listen to or tell the story of **The king's birthday music** (*track 28*) and encourage the children to join in by drumming palms on knees when the music is loud, and finger tapping on knees when the music becomes quiet.

- Talk with the children about the two kinds of footwear in the story and show them examples of clogs and fabric slippers.

- Ask the children to pull on invisible wooden clogs. Are they heavy? Invite them to tell you what they would feel like. Try the invisible silk slippers – how would it feel to dance in them.

- Now let the children move about in a large space in their invisible wooden shoes, so that their feet make heavy, loud sounds as they walk. Sit down again and change them for invisible silk slippers, moving softly and lightly about the space.

- Play **Drumming music** (*track 29*) and ask the children to dance to the loud and quiet drum music in their imaginary shoes.

I hear the band

- Listen to *I hear the band* (*track 30*):

I hear the band far away, far away, far away,
I hear the band far away, far away, far away.

I hear the band near the town, near the town,
near the town...

I hear the band marching by, marching by,
marching by...

I hear the band leave the town, leave the town,
leave the town...

I hear the band far away, far way, far away,
I hear the band far away, far way, far away.

- Talk about the music getting louder as the band gets nearer, and quieter as the players march away again. Can the children think of other sounds that do this? (*Police sirens, ice-cream van chimes...*) Sing the song with the CD, matching the changing volume.

- Ask a few volunteers to accompany the song without the CD, using drums or soundmakers. The drummers match the volume of the singing as it gets louder and then quieter.

- Record and play back the performance. Can the children say if the drummers matched the singers? Can the performance be improved?

Our senses

Musical focus: *Timbre*   **Area of learning:** *Creative development*

YELLOW

RESOURCES
A biscuit for
each child.

TUNE
G G A G
What can you see?

What can you see?

- Everyone listens to *What can you see?* (*track 31*), joining in with
  the echoed first lines and actions when they are familiar:

  What can you *see*?   *(hand on brow as if searching)*
  What can you *see*?
  I can *see* the pattern of the waves on the sea.

  What can you *hear*?   *(hands cupped behind ears)*
  What can you *hear*?
  I can *hear* the seagulls when they're flying near.

  What can you *smell*?   *(thumb and first finger pinching nose)*
  What can you *smell*?
  I can *smell* the salt that's hiding in a shell.

  What can you *feel*?   *(foot rubbing on floor)*
  What can you *feel*?
  I can *feel* the stones moving under my heel.

  What can you *taste*?   *(lick pretend ice-cream)*
  What can you *taste*?
  I can *taste* my ice-cream, couldn't bear to let it waste.

- Ask the children if they know where the song is set, and talk about
  their experiences of the seaside.

- Talk about the senses, noticing that each verse is about using one
  of them. Give each child a biscuit and let them look at its shape,
  listen to the sound of breaking it in two, smell its flavour, feel its
  texture, then finally taste it.

BLUE

RESOURCES
Items associated
with the seaside.

Access to a
computer to use
the interactive
seaside picture
on the CD-
ROM.

Seaside soundmakers

- Show the children a collection of seaside items, eg
    - seashells;
    - pebbles;
    - ice-cream cone;
    - beach ball;
    - bucket and spade;
    - seagull's feather.

- Spend some time investigating the items, using your different
  senses: looking at shapes, feeling textures, listening to how they
  sound when tapped or rubbed, smelling the saltiness on some of
  them, and if appropriate sampling their taste.

- Listen to *Seaside sounds* (*track 32*) or let the children play with the
  interactive seaside picture on the CD-ROM (*click on items to hear
  their sound*). Talk about the sounds and match them to items in
  your seaside collection.

- Help the children find different ways of using their voices to make
  seaside sounds: swishing waves, licking icecreams, bouncing ball,
  seagull mews, etc.

GREEN

TIP
When the children are familiar with the conversation, ask individuals to take turns at being leader

Uncle Chain Maker

- You play the leader and the children select a child to be Uncle Chain Maker. Everyone joins hands to make a long chain with the leader at one end and Uncle at the other. The leader and Uncle Chain Maker have a conversation in loud voices (*reference track 33*):

Leader: Hey, Uncle Chain Maker.

Uncle: Yes.

Leader: Do you want to make a chain?

Uncle: Yes.

Leader: Daddy's brought some things from the sea.

Uncle: Yes.

Leader: Chickpeas and raisins.

Uncle: Yes.

Leader: So eat first and then come home, making sounds like –

Uncle: – the waves at sea *(Uncle makes an extended vocal sound like waves)*

- Uncle Chain Maker continues making his sound of the sea, and the others join in.

- Uncle Chain Maker and the child holding his hand raise their arms to make an arch. The leader walks under bringing the rest of the chain, all making Uncle's sound of the sea.

- When everyone is through the arch, the chain breaks, Uncle Chain Maker's partner takes his place and the activity begins again. This time Uncle makes a different vocal seaside sound which the other children imitate. Help children explore a range of seaside sounds such as: sand being scooped by a spade, lilo being blown up, beach ball bounced, speed boat whooshing past and so on.

GREY

RESOURCES
Access to a sandy play area and a collection of seaside items.

Cassette recorder.

Seaside symphony

- In small groups, take the children to the 'seaside' – the sandy play area of your setting. Gather in it a collection of seaside items, eg beach ball, bucket and spade, seashells, a water tray, pebbles, toy boats, sun hats, and so on.

- Talk with the children about the vocal sounds they have made to represent those heard at the seaside and encourage them to explore the sounds they can make with the things in the 'seaside' area:

  - swilling and pouring water;
  - digging and patting with the bucket and spade;
  - beachball: blowing it up, patting and bouncing it;
  - shaking handfuls of seashells;
  - vocal hums and 'whooshes' for boats;
  - seagull mews.

- Make a cassette recording of the sounds made at the 'seaside', and play them back at story time as an introduction to a story about your day at the sea.

- Give everyone an ice-cream.

Our senses

Musical focus: *Timbre*   **Area of learning:** *Creative development*

YELLOW

TUNE
B E G# E
The clock goes tick

The clock goes tick tock

• Listen to *The clock goes tick tock* (*track 34*) and join in singing the words, and making yawning and stretching actions:

The clock goes tick tock, the clock goes tick tock,
The clock goes tick tock, it's time to stretch and yawn.
   Stretch and yawn, stretch and yawn,
The clock goes tick tock, it's time to stretch and yawn.

• Ask the children for suggestions of other verses to sing which describe the actions they make and sounds they hear when they wake up early in the morning, eg

   – 'it's time to brush your teeth: 'brush brush brush brush...';

   – 'it's time to wash your face';

   – 'it's time to polish your shoes'.

• Sing the new verses with or without the CD backing track (*track 35*), adding actions and appropriate vocal sounds.

BLUE

RESOURCES
A clock face with moving hands or a copy of the template provided on the CD-ROM.

TIP
Some children may be able to make the tick-tock sound on a wood block or other instrument.

Watch the clock

• Use a large clock face with turning hands (*or the cut out provided on the CD-ROM*) and talk about the sound a grandfather clock makes as the hands go round. Demonstrate the hands turning on the clock and make a vocal 'tick tock' sound. Invite the children to join in.

• Talk about what the children do at different times of day and select three suggestions, ending with 'bed time', eg

   – seven o'clock: stretch and yawn;

   – one o'clock: eat your lunch;

   – four o'clock: play bounce a ball

   – eight o'clock: bed time.

• All together make an action and vocal sound for each of the suggestions ensuring that all the children are familiar with them. Everyone pretends to sleep and snore at bed time.

• Make up a short piece of music using the ticking clock and vocal sounds and actions:

   – all say 'tick tock' as you turn the hands of the clock round to seven o'clock;

   – all make stretching and yawning actions and vocal sounds;

   – all say 'tick tock' again as the hands turn to one o'clock;

   – all make munching actions and sounds, and so on until bed time.

What can you hear?

• Listen to *What can you hear?* (*track 36, tune: What shall we do with the drunken sailor*) and join in singing the words as they become familiar:

What can you hear when you wake up yawning?
What can you hear when you wake up yawning?
What can you hear when you wake up yawning?
   I can hear the milkman.

What can you hear when you make your dinner...
   I can hear the pots and pans.

What can you hear when you play in the garden...
   I can hear the birds sing.

What can you hear when you're ready for bedtime...
   I can hear the clock chime.

• With the children, explore a variety of appropriate instruments and soundmakers to accompany each verse, eg

   – milk bottles: tap tambourine jingles;

   – pots and pans: tap cymbals with a hard beater;

   – birdsong: make vocal sounds and whistles;

   – clock: tap a chime bar.

All in a day

• Remind the children of the sounds they found for each verse of the song (*see above*).

• Put together a grand performance of *The clock goes tick tock* and *What can you hear?* using vocal sounds, actions and instruments:

   – move the hands of the clock round the face, all making 'tick tock' sounds together until seven o'clock: 'It's time to stretch and yawn'.

   – sing *What can you hear?* accompanying it with your instrumental sounds;

   – move the hands of the clock again until 'It's time to each your lunch', then sing 'What can you hear when you eat your dinner', and so on through the day, ending with the chiming of the clock for bed time.

Our senses

Musical focus: *Timbre*   Area of learning: *Creative development*

YELLOW

RESOURCES
Large board or length of strong fabric and a wide range of sound sources which may be attached to the backing.

TIP
Parents could contribute with objects from home.

Encourage children to talk about the actions they use to make a sound such as tapping, scraping, rubbing, shaking and so on

Make a sound wall

- Create a sound wall with the children by firmly sewing, stapling or gluing a range of interesting objects that can be used as sound sources to a large board or stiff fabric. Include things such as crinkly paper, corrugated paper, bubblewrap, sandpaper, velcro, zips, velvet, silk, strings of pasta and large beads, bells, milk bottle tops, shells, plastic egg boxes, tinfoil dishes.

- Keep a variety of beaters handy such as wooden, metal and plastic spoons and forks, pastry brush, strip of cardboard, pencil and ruler, etc, so that the children may explore sounds by tapping, and scraping as well as by touching.

- Encourage children to explore sounds whenever they can, talking to them about the actions they use to make the sounds.

BLUE

RESOURCES
Duplicates of soundmakers from the sound wall.

TUNE
  G E F G
What can you play?

TIP
Encourage the children to talk about the material from which the sound maker is made such as wood, metal, plastic and so on.

What can you play?

- Sit in a circle with a selection of sound sources from the sound wall in the centre.

- Listen to **What can you play** (*track 37*).

What can you play? What can you play?
I can play my special sound in this way.

- At the end of the song, one child selects a sound source from the centre of the circle, takes it back to her place and makes a sound on it whilst the other children watch and listen carefully. The practitioner talks with the children about the way in which the sound was made, such as by tapping, shaking, rubbing, scraping and so on.

- The child returns the soundmaker to the centre of the circle and the activity is repeated until every child has had a turn at making a sound.

- Encourage the children to join in singing when they are ready.

GREEN

RESOURCES
A collection of sound sources such as crinkly paper, corrugated paper, strings of pasta and large beads, bells, plastic egg box or tinfoil dishes.

TIP
Ask individual children to take turns as leader.

Play it - change it

• The children stand in a space where they can see and hear the practitioner. The practitioner chooses a soundmaker and makes a sound by tapping, shaking, rubbing, blowing or scraping it at the end of the first line of the chant. The soundmaker is passed to a child who then plays a different sound at the end of the second line of the chant:

Please look at me and hear what I play, –

leader plays a sound then passes the soundmaker to someone else

Then play something else in a different way. –

next person plays a different sound with the soundmaker

• Say the rhyme again and invite another child to use a different action to make a sound on the same soundmaker. When the possibilities for that soundmaker have all been tried, change to a new one.

• Explore at least two different ways of making sounds on each sound source.

GREY

RESOURCES
Large selection of soundmakers from the sound wall (YELLOW).

TUNE
  A   F♯ F♯ F♯
There was a man

Aiken Drum

• Listen to the song, *Aiken Drum* (*track 38*), joining in with actions suggested by the instruments that Aiken Drum plays, and with the words of the song as they become familiar:

Chorus: There was a man lived in the moon,
        lived in the moon, lived in the moon,
     There was a man lived in the moon,
        and his name was Aiken Drum.

Verse: And he played upon a ladle,
        a ladle, a ladle,
     He played upon a ladle,
        and his name was Aiken Drum.

     And he played upon a teacup...

     And he played upon a saucepan lid...

• All stand in a circle. In the centre, place a large selection of soundmakers from the sound wall. One child stands in the centre of the circle which represents the moon. All sing the chorus of *Aiken Drum*, while the child selects a soundmaker. 'Aiken Drum' plays during the verse, while the other children sing and copy the playing action, eg

     And she played some crinkly paper...

• 'Aiken Drum' selects the next child to play, and the activity continues. (*Use backing track 39 if required.*)

Our senses

Musical focus: *Timbre*   **Area of learning:** *Creative development*

YELLOW

RESOURCES
A glove puppet.
A sheet of paper for every child.

TUNE
G B A G
Eve - ry -bo - dy

TIP
Parents could contribute with objects from home.

Encourage children to talk about the actions they use to make a sound such as tapping, scraping, rubbing, shaking, etc.

Everybody do this

- Introduce children to a welcoming glove puppet who can make different sounds with a largish piece of paper. While the puppet makes different sounds by shaking, waving and tapping the paper, the children copy the actions with their hands. As they become more confident in following the puppet's actions, the children copy the sounds with their own pieces of paper.

- Play *Everybody do it* (*track 40*). The puppet accompanies the song with a paper sound and the children join in with their own pieces of paper.

Everybody do this, do this, do this,
Everybody do this just like me.

- Repeat the song several times, using as many different kinds of paper and ways of playing that the puppet can think of and the children can copy.

BLUE

RESOURCES
A glove puppet.
A wide variety of paper types.

TUNE
G B A G
Eve - ry -bo - dy

EXTENSION
Record some of the children's paper sounds on a cassette recorder. As everyone listens to the recording, children offer to copy the sound 'live' on an appropriate piece of paper.

It's your turn to do it

- The children sit in a circle with a selection of different kinds of paper such as newspaper, tissue paper, thin card, greaseproof, wrapping paper and so on, laid out in the centre.

- While you/the glove puppet hand one of the pieces of paper to one of the children, sing:

(Carlie's) turn to do this, do this, do this,
(Carlie's) turn to do this just like me.

- The chosen child makes a sound with the paper. Decide together how the sound is being made, eg tearing, and all sing the song with the new words and with the child accompanying:

This is how you tear it, tear it, tear it,
This is how you tear it, just like me.

- Repeat the song with another child choosing a different way of making a sound. Continue in this way until several sounds have been explored and used to accompany new verses of the song. Encourage the children to copy the sound action while they sing.

GREEN

RESOURCES
A wide variety of paper types.

A print out of the CD-ROM picture.

TIP
Make a cassette recording of the sounds as you find them during your walk.

Sound walk

- Explore a variety of sounds which can be made with different types of paper and card. Show the children the sound walk picture (CD-ROM). Talk about the sounds they would hear if they were the children in the picture.

- Outdoors, lead the children on a sound walk to discover sounds that could be represented by a variety of paper sound sources, handled in different ways when they return indoors. These could include leaves being scuffed, feet tiptoeing, light breeze, gusty wind, raindrops, coats swishing and so on.

- Indoors in a large space, the children sit in a circle with a selection of different kinds of paper laid out in the centre. The children recall their sound walk and find ways of imitating their favourite sounds by choosing from the variety of paper.

- Everyone has a small item made of paper that they can wear or hold. The children set off again on the sound walk, but this time create their own sounds with paper to accompany the journey.

GREY

RESOURCES
A sheet of newspaper for every child.

Paper poem

- Say the first part of the poem while the children make paper sounds to illustrate the words. When the poem is familiar, some children may wish to work on their own.

I shake my paper gently – it sounds like the wind,
I tap it with my fingertips, and hear the rain begin.
Folding, smoothing, make it flat,
Now I wear it as a hat.

Then scrunching like a _____
And tearing, ripping _____
It floats, it falls just like a _____
Landing quietly on the floor.

- Find different endings to the second part of the poem, encouraging the children to use their imaginations to create their own ideas and sounds.

- Make a grand final performance of the whole poem with paper sounds. Children with streamers and costumes of crepe paper could add movements to bring the poem to life.

Our senses

Musical focus: *Timbre*   **Area of learning:** *Creative development*

YELLOW

VIDEOCLIPS
Reference clips of the YELLOW, BLUE, GREEN and GREY activities are included on the CD-ROM.

RESOURCES
A sugar shaker, egg whisk, cake tin and wooden spoon.

TUNE
D E F# D
I hear shak - ing

TIP
Talk about the actions uses to make a sound such as tapping, scraping, rubbing, shaking and so on.

Cake for tea

• Talk with the children about a variety of kitchen utensils used in making cakes – whisks, sugar shakers, wooden spoons and cake tins. Show them these utensils.

• Listen to *Cake for tea* (*track 41*) and identify which utensil appears in each verse of the song. (*Sugar shaker, egg whisk, wooden spoon.*)

I hear shaking... *(sugar shaker)*

I hear whisking... *(whisk)*

I hear tapping... *(wooden spoon and cake tin)*

BLUE

RESOURCES
Kitchen utensils as above.

TIP
Encourage children to talk about the material from which the sound maker is made such as wood, metal, plastic and so on.

Cake for tea – actions

• Explore the shapes, textures and materials of the utensils and ask children to investigate the sounds they can make by shaking, turning or tapping them.

• Ask the children to watch and then copy you as you make shaking, turning or tapping hand actions one after the other.

• All join in singing the song with or without the CD (*track 41*). Encourage the children to copy you as you make shaking, turning and tapping actions during the song:

Leader: I hear shaking,
What can it be?
Shaking sugar in the bowl,
Cake for tea.

I hear whisking,
What can it be?
Whisking eggs into the bowl,
Cake for tea.

I hear tapping,
What can it be?
Tap it all into the tin,
Cake for tea.

All: I hear shaking,
What can it be?
Shaking sugar in the bowl,
Cake for tea.

I hear whisking,
What can it be?
Whisking eggs into the bowl,
Cake for tea.

I hear tapping,
What can it be?
Tap it all into the tin,
Cake for tea.

Cake makers

GREEN

RESOURCES
Cooking utensils.

TUNE
E F G E
I have sounds one

TIP
Some children may be able to find their own sounds and take the role of the practitioner in the activity.

EXTENSION
Increase the number of hidden sounds to three and sing, 'I have sounds, one two three...'

I have sounds one and two

- All sit in a circle with two cooking utensils, such as a cheese grater and a cake tin. Demonstrate how you can tap the cake tin or scrape the cheese grater with a wooden spoon. Ask the children to make tapping and scraping actions respectively as you demonstrate each.

- Hide the utensils behind a screen or in a box. Sing the song, *I have sounds* (*track 42, tune: Tommy Thumb*):

> I have sounds one and two
> Hide away.
> Listen now, carefully,
> Which shall I play?

- As the song finishes, select one of the utensils, ensuring that the children cannot see it. Ask the children to listen carefully to the sound you make with **the** utensil, and identify it by making a tapping or a scraping action with their hands.

GREY

RESOURCES
Tambourine, wood block and scraper.

TUNE
D   D D C
Shake, sha-ke-ty

TIP
Give opportunities for everyone to accompany a verse.

The sounds may be made all through each verse, or just on the sound words (shake, tap or scrape etc). Try both and let the children decide which they prefer.

Shake, tappety, scrape

- Listen to *Shake, tappety, scrape* (*track 43*):

> Shake, shakety, shake,
> Shake, shakety, shake,
> Shake, shakety, shake,
> Shake, shakety, shake.
> This is how we play the tambourine,
> Shake, shakety, shake.
>
> Tap, tappety, tap...
> This is how we play the wood block...
>
> Scrape, scrapety, scrape...
> This is how we play the scraper...
>
> Shake, tappety, scrape...
> This is how we play the instruments...

- Talk about how each instrument is played on the recording. All copy the actions of playing with your hands as you listen again.

- Select one child to play a tambourine while everyone sings the first verse and joins in with playing actions. Sing the second verse with a different child playing a wood block, and so on with the third verse accompanied by a scraper. Then all combined.

- Move out of doors or into a large space for a final performance. Three children play the instruments, while the others sing and make whole body dance movements, shaking their bodies, tapping their feet, and making large scraping gestures with their arms.

Our senses

Musical focus: *Timbre* **Area of learning:** *Creative development*

YELLOW

Teddy bear, teddy bear

- Listen to *Teddy bear, teddy bear* (*track 44*) and join in with the actions as they become familiar:

Teddy bear, teddy bear, touch your nose,   (*touch nose with finger*)

Teddy bear, teddy bear, touch your toes,   (*touch toes with fingers*)

Teddy bear, teddy bear, touch the ground,   (*touch ground with palm of hand*)

Teddy bear, teddy bear, turn around,   (*rotate hand*)

Teddy Bear, teddy bear, climb up stairs,   (*walk hands up stairs*)

Teddy bear, teddy bear, say your prayers   (*bow head and shoulders*)

Teddy Bear, teddy bear, turn off the light,   (*flick index finger*)

Teddy bear, teddy bear, wave goodnight.   (*small, sleepy wave*)

BLUE

Teddy bear, teddy bear – play the beat

RESOURCES
A wide variety of instruments.

TIP
Invite parents to share the experience: joining in the song, or being an audience.

Enjoy the silence of 'say your prayers'.

- Everyone chants *Teddy bear, teddy bear* (*track 44*) joining in with the actions until all are familiar.

- Perform one of teddy's actions to a steady beat, such as:

touch   your   toes,   touch   your   toes...

Encourage the children to join in. Try other teddy actions, such as 'climb upstairs'.

- Explain that teddy's actions in the song are like the actions we use to play instruments, eg

  - touch your nose, eg tap finger on a tambourine;
  - touch your toes, eg tap a woodblock;
  - touch the ground, eg a firm strike with flat palm on tambour;
  - turn around, eg rotate a cabasa or swirl maraca;
  - climb upstairs, eg play from low to high on a xylophone;
  - say your prayers – keep silent;
  - turn off the light, eg flick a jingle or cymbal;
  - wave goodnight, eg gently shake a tambourine.

- Play the beat on as many different instruments as teddy's actions suggest.

- While some children say the chant, others accompany by playing the beat on a variety of instruments using the actions you have explored together.

Teddy's day out

- Chant *Teddy bear, teddy bear* (*track 44*) together and remind the children about ways in which teddy's actions in the song can be used to make sounds on instruments.

- Talk with the children about how teddy might feel during a visit to a playground (*eg happy, excited, shy*), or at the arrival of a new baby in the family (*eg excited, anxious, proud*).

- Encourage the children to create expressive actions and sounds on the instruments they have explored to illustrate teddy's feelings, eg

    – play short, light, jerky sounds for the excitement of the new baby coming home;

    – slow, quiet, gentle sounds for tiptoeing around the house when the baby sleeps;

    – quick brisk marching sounds to accompany the first walk outside with the pushchair.

Teddy bears' picnic

- Show the children the storyboard of a teddy bears' picnic. With your support and guidance, encourage the children to explore sounds to describe the main events and how the teddies felt. (*Use a wide range of instruments and soundmakers and encourage the children to employ the playing techniques they explored in* BLUE *level.*)

Include:

    – setting the scene: sounds as the picnic hamper is packed – clanking cutlery, watery sounds as drinks are made, baby's squeaky toys being packed;

    – enjoying the picnic: crunching crisps, wobbling jelly, wasps buzzing near the sandwiches, gentle breeze and maybe a hint of rain, taps of bat and ball games, running up and down hills;

    – arriving home: tired footsteps to bed, brushing teeth, snuggling under the covers, kisses goodnight.

- Record the three scenes of picnic music and play them back while displaying each picture in turn.

Index

Music, songs, stories, chants and raps

Audio CD track lists (CD 1 and CD 2)

CD 1

CD 2